Reflections of Fate

COPYRIGHT © 2016 PJ Barns

For my mum who sadly passed away just before I could publish my very first novel.

I hope she is proud of her son's achievement as she looks down on us all

Thank you my wife

Contents

Chapter 1 4
Chapter 2 14
Chapter 3 31
Chapter 4 50
Chapter 5 66
Chapter 6 76
Chapter 7 87
Chapter 8 97
Chapter 9 106
Chapter 10 111
Chapter 11 125
Chapter 12 153
Chapter 13 167
Chapter 14 195
Chapter 15 210
Chapter 16 217
Chapter 17 240
Chapter 18 250
Chapter 19 256
Chapter 20 266
Chapter 21 275

Chapter 1

The auction room was a little chilly with its high ceilings and tiled flooring, but Alison didn't mind in the slightest. After walking around, browsing amongst the items for sale, she soon warmed up. Alison and her husband, John, had taken their time strolling around and browsing; after all, it was a weekend away in this sleepy little village of Hamilton in Hampshire. Both were of the same mind to spend the time with a bit of relaxing, moochig around the village, and a nice pub lunch, just right for a rainy Sunday morning.

With nothing in particular to look for or buy, they both wandered about aimlessly, picking up this and that: a small silver snuff box, a mother of pearl beaded hair brush. What they'd found was okay, but nothing had jumped out at Alison as a "must have" item or a hidden treasure. She looked across at John. He was thumbing through a pile of old music magazines with an intent look on his face, and she knew he would be there a while, engrossed in the magazines. At thirty-eight years of age, he was not old, but he did like collecting old things as a hobby, and being an accountant, he had the money to indulge his likes without impinging on her income as a teacher.

As she meandered about, Alison looked off to her side, noting a plain full-length mirror with a lightly carved dark wood surround. It was nothing special, but it caught her eye because she remembered the last time she'd been getting ready to go out and how she'd struggled with her small dressing table mirror in their bedroom. It had been a nightmare! Remembering this, she turned to her auction schedule and noted the number, lot 351. In her mind, Alison fixed a rough price of £50, which would be her guide limit. Otherwise, she might as well just buy one from the shop or even online.

After another round of browsing through tat and expensive items alike, trying to find more bargains, Alison was caught up by John in the small narrow maze of things waiting to be gathered up and fought over, and together, they strolled into the main hall. The actual auction room wasn't that full when they went through, but they sat down near the back anyway. Alison and John had only a couple of items each to look out for, her first one being lot 219, a silver charm for her charm bracelet. Although it looked okay, it wasn't an important buy, and she'd decided on a limit of £25 for the little teddy bear figure.

The bidding opened at £5 and seemed quite brisk, soon getting to £9. Alison waited a little to see who was interested. A large lady at the front of the room shot her hand up. "We have £10," the auctioneer called out. The generous lady looked relaxed, as if she knew what she was doing, and sat there in her tweed skirt and large cable knit jumper, her arms folded in front of her as if she had a grump on about something. To Alison, she looked to be around the fifty-year-old mark, and Alison instantly judged the woman as a likely candidate for wanting the teddy bear charm possibly more than her.

Alison's focus quickly drew back to the auctioneer calling out, "£15... £17... £19." Two other women were now bidding. One woman was nearer Alison's age of thirty-six, and the other was a bit younger, maybe in her twenties, and she joined in the bidding process eagerly. The larger woman seemed the danger, though, upping her bid with a wave to £20. Alison now entered the proceedings with a slight rise of her hand and took the bidding to £22, but when the other women immediately outbid her with bids of £24 and £25, she bowed out, keeping her powder dry for her next interest. The little silver charm finally went to the large woman in the front for £31, as Alison had guessed earlier in the process would be the case, but she was not too concerned.

John's interest was next, and it turned out that he was the

only bidder for the pile of old music magazines, so that was okay. Very soon, the auctioneer slammed down the gavel: "SOLD! Ten pounds to the gentleman in the green jacket." John gave his full name as Mr John Fisher and his auction number, 67. John's purchase completed, Alison now completely focused, waiting for her mirror. She knew it wouldn't be too long now, and John, happy with his bargain, decided to go and buy them both a coffee so that Alison didn't miss the auction. It was lucky that he did because, just as he was returning to his seat, carrying the two coffees, the auctioneer announced, "LOT 351!" After describing the mirror as unusual and probably nineteenth century, with some charming, non-pretentious carving around the frame and in good condition, the auctioneer bellowed, "Will anyone start me off with £20?" Alison looked about, and seeing John returning with the hot drinks, she gave him a smile, thinking, *It's always nice to have him around, even if he doesn't always say or do anything.* He was her unvarying support.

A hand went up at the front of the room again, but this time, it was an oriental-looking guy, and another hand went up to Alison's left, another guy, slim and balding. Once the bidding had inched its way up to £35, Alison put her hand up to indicate £40, which was nodded at by the auctioneer. But then he asked, "Do I hear £45?" The room fell silent, and Alison held her breath, but Mr Oriental at the front raised his hand again and announced £42. Alison cursed under her breath and, not wanting to appear too eager, paused for a few heartbeats before raising her hand and upping her bid to £45. There was another nod from the auctioneer. The guy to her left, Mr Baldy, shook his head when asked if he wanted to take the bid to £47, but Mr Prawn Cracker had other ideas and raised his hand. He was now her only rival.

The bid now stood at £47. Alison took a deep breath and stuck out her chest, even if it wasn't a particularly significant one, to show she was getting competitive and determined to win, especially after missing out on the little silver teddy charm. Her hand flicked up, and £50 was her bid as her eyes bore into the back of Mr Oriental's head. She gritted her teeth, daring him to make another attempt. There was silence. Then more silence. The auctioneer looked at Mr Oriental and said to the room, "The bid is at £50?" Silence. "Selling at £50 for this delightful mirror... Selling twice at £50. Do I hear £51, anyone?" He craned his neck to peer around the room and then glanced back at the Asian guy at the front of the room again, who, thankfully, shook his head.

Alison sucked in a big mouthful of air. Her heart was beating as if she were bidding hundreds of pounds, and she was absolutely thrilled when she realised Mr Chow Mein had given up.

She had won, and the auctioneer was announcing into the room, "Selling to the lady at the back in the white jumper." BANG! "SOLD for fifty pounds! Name please?"

"Alison Fisher. Number 68," she blurted out in a shrill voice.

Alison rushed to fetch their purchases, so great was her excitement, while John collected their Audi Estate car. He backed it up to the loading area and then, with the help of a burly warehouse worker, managed to fit the mirror and magazines into the car comfortably, joking about not breaking the mirror and, of course, the resulting seven years bad luck.

John wasn't a muscular chap, but he stayed reasonably trim with some exercise at the gym once or twice a week and also a game of squash with Richard Blake, his friend from work. Standing at around six feet tall, he had to stoop to get the mirror into his car, bumping his head slightly on the protruding tailgate as he and the warehouse worker struggled with Alison's large purchase. John simply brushed his dark ruffled hair back into position with his hand. *The beauty of having short hair*, he thought.

Alison slid into the passenger side of the car and slipped the seat belt on so that it sat neatly between her breasts. The thought often came to mind that the action made them look like they jutted out as much as they had when she was in her twenties, and even though they weren't very large, she could at least feel proud of them for the duration of a car journey. The soft white tight jumper she was wearing felt a little warm now that she was in the car. Although it was only early September, it was rainy, cloudy, and dull, certainly jumper weather during her stroll around the back of the auction room. She had been glad of it, that was for sure.

Finally, after wrestling with the mirror, slamming the tailgate, and thanking the warehouse worker for his help, John opened the driver's door and jumped into the seat. Alison noted he wore his jeans today, which always looked a little strange to her, as he wore a suit all week for work, but as is often the case when one looks relaxed, he seemed to feel comfortable in them. Starting the engine, they headed off to the Jack Rabbit Pub, though now it would be to eat lunch and not their original plan of brunch, having spent longer at the auction than anticipated.

Pulling up outside, they parked quickly around the back of the pub, where it shared a carpark with a Mercedes dealership. Before exiting the car, Alison asked, "Is that stuff going to be okay there in the back of the car?" indicating with a flick of her head the new purchases in the back of the car, which were in full view of anyone passing by.

John dismissed the small concern, saying, "Yeah, they're fine, babe. I can't see some scroats trying to run off with your mirror unless they're built like Schwarzenegger." Both smiling at his response, they quickly left the car and entered the rear door of the pub, which was just a few yards' stroll. They weren't locals to the pub, but they had been there quite a few times, so they knew what they had to do to get served, which also helped make it feel homely to them. John went to the bar first as Alison grabbed a table near the open fire – so cosy and so relaxing.

John came back to the table with his pint of lager, a glass of dry white wine for her, and a large green wine bottle with a wooden spoon sticking out of the top that had the number twelve on it to show the staff which food order they were. They scanned the menu and ordered their food, settling on just having a roast dinner each with no starter. After all, it was only supposed to be a stop on the way home. An evening meal would be their focus later when Rich Blake and his wife, Tanya, popped around to spend the evening with them.

Alison could not wait to show Tanya her new mirror. *Pity I didn't get the charm too*, she thought, *but ah, well, never mind*.

John broke through her thoughts, almost reading her mindset, saying, "Can't wait to show Rich my music mags." And then he asked, "Are you pleased with your mirror then, darling?"

"Yes," she said, "very! It's one of those things I really wanted. A full-length mirror in the bedroom to check how I look when getting ready to go out, but it's not been a priority, so I haven't got one up till now. So, yes, I'm pleased. It will fit neatly to the right of the dressing table in the corner of the bedroom." Then she paused, a stray thought crossing her mind. Chancing her arm, she added, "Could be a little kinky, a mirror at the end of the bed?"

John reacted in a disappointing way to her suggestion, with a simple shrug and a "Hmm, yeah," and as he did so often these days, he changed the subject, this time to wondering how long the food was going to be. Alison's mind was now dwelling on the non-answer just given. Their sex life had noticeably deteriorated to maybe once a month, and even then, it just didn't seem the same.

She had confided in Rich Blake's wife, Tanya, who had become her close friend of late, asking her if she thought he might be straying, to which Tanya had replied, "No, I doubt it, but there's no way I'd know for sure, I'm afraid."

"But he just seems to be off it," Alison had mused. She had tried hard to get him going again, dressing up in sexy lingerie, leaving the TV on sex-themed films or TV programs, and giving him a sexy calendar for his garage. She had even offered a blowjob when he'd said he was too tired for full sex (again). *It's a good job I have a sex toy*, she'd thought. What with that and the "power shower," at least it had kept her from pouncing on the postman or something. Tanya had reassured her that it might just be a phase thing or something or maybe his work had taken its toll so Alison should just relax on it and try not to pressure him. Fingers crossed, it would sort itself out eventually.

The roasts arrived, and they were soon tucking in. Alison's mind was now thinking of eating her meal, and she was eager to get home and get the mirror into position to see how it looked.

Chapter 2

John had laboured to get the mirror into the car, and he knew he would struggle like mad to get it out, but he and Alison hoped that with a bit of luck, a couple of students, Lee and Stephen from next door, would be there when they arrived back at their house.

As they pulled into the drive, to their relief, the two lads were outside their home messing around with a football in their driveway. They weren't bad lads and didn't baulk at the idea of helping John get the somewhat heavy mirror into the house and upstairs. Alison couldn't help smiling, giving a little smirk to the lads when they joked, with a wink, about the mirror's role in the bedroom. Moreover, with the innuendos flying about, Alison thought the lads were a little flirty with her, and she couldn't help but feel a little flattered with them being only nineteen and twenty-one years old. They were being purposely cheeky to see not only John's reaction, but hers too. Lee, the elder of the two, had started it by saying things like, "No problem helping, Mrs Fisher, as long as we're not sticking it up on the ceiling?" Then Stephen joined in with, "You will have to be careful it doesn't rock and fall over at a vital moment, as it only has little feet. Mrs Fisher, you only have little feet; do you rock about too?"

The lads guffawed at their silly jokes, so much so that John jumped in, saying, "Yeah, yeah, lads. You drop this, and you will have swollen feet. Now stop messing about." Alison loved it all, really; they were like the sons she never had. Even when berating them for the loud music they played, they were always respectful and turned it down straight away when asked, replying with, "Sorry, Mrs Fisher, anything for you." Their long-suffering but brilliant mum, Tina, was always complaining that they, with their smelly socks and even more stinking breath, were eating her out of house and home and that Alison was welcome to them. She would even pay her to take them off her hands!

Through the entrance hall and up the stairs went the mirror, then along the landing and on to the second door on the left. Alison opened it and watched her mirror make its way into the bedroom. Lee jibed again, "Ahhh, this is the inner sanctum where all the action is. Where do you want it, Mrs Fisher?" This was quickly followed by, "And the mirror?" Stephen, acting now as his comedy partner, followed in with, "If it's not going on the ceiling, do you want it at the bottom of the bed so you can see Mr Fisher over your shoulder?"

"Hey! Careful!" Alison exclaimed. She didn't mind a bit of banter, but it was stepping over the line now, and she didn't want John getting cross at the comments. To stop it completely, she took control and pointed over at the corner of the room, near the bottom of the bed and to the side, so that she could get a complete look at herself while her whole body was bathed in the natural light coming across from the window to the right of her.

When finally in place, they all paused a second. John, puffing and panting as he got his breath back, managed to thank the cheeky students, telling them, "There are some beers in the fridge. Grab a couple each for yourselves, lads; we really appreciate your help." They swaggered out of the room, pleased with getting a couple of beers and in the good books of the "MILF" next door for just ten minutes of work. Mrs Fisher was their "Mrs Robinson".

Later that evening, John and Alison were getting ready for their visitors, Rich and Tanya. Alison was busy in the kitchen getting nibbles ready while John got the ice for the drinks, also nipping to the shop for garlic bread and a few other bits and pieces. The plan was they would provide the nibbles and the venue, while Rich and Tanya brought the wine, and then, when Alison and John were over to the other couple's house the next time, of course, the roles would be reversed. With the couple of wines they already had, the evening was set to be relaxed.

They normally had Chinese food or pizza delivered from town for their meal, and although they had eaten earlier at the pub, they were unperturbed; it would be nearer 8:00 pm that evening until they would have to eat a full meal again. For John, this was never a problem if pizza was involved, and although their house was just outside of Southampton, just as it started to get rural, it was still close enough to get good take-away service.

Now, with all the preparation done, John was showering while Alison grabbed at different dresses, tops, and blouses, holding them up and looking at how they hung on her in her new mirror. As she gazed at her reflection, she noticed a mark or smudge on the mirror surface, but as she looked more closely, it seemed to be condensation or something. Alison breathed on it to increase its area and definition and recognised the figures 351. She remembered it was the lot number from the auction house. Believing it to be just a mark from the temporary lot number, she grabbed a piece of clothing and wiped it off easily, thinking to herself it had probably been written on the glass at one point as well as on the tag tied to it on the side. Then Alison realised the lot 351 tag was still tied on the side, so she leant across and pulled it off.

Next thing she knew, she was waking up on the floor, her

head spinning and her stomach nauseous, the paper tag still in her right hand. She hadn't hurt herself in the fall and, wrapped only in her big bath towel, she slowly picked herself up as John rushed in from the shower looking concerned and quizzical.

"What the bloody hell happened? Why were you on the floor? Are you okay?" he asked.

"I don't know," she replied. "I think I must have fainted or something, or maybe I just moved too quickly." She put the tag to the side and stumbled to their en-suite shower room to sit on the toilet. She shook her head and tested her balance, but she didn't feel too bad, just puzzled more than anything as to why it had happened, and she certainly didn't feel the need not to carry on with a shower. John insisted she leave the door open, just in case, and to keep the temperature a little lower than when she normally took her showers. She thought it a good idea and felt confident that if she did feel faint again, he could rush in and stop her from hurting herself.

Alison eased herself into the shower with no problem at all. In fact, she was now feeling fine, just mystified by her previous episode. Her mind played over the sudden spell, but as the warm water cascaded down her tense body, she gave an audible sigh and soon turned her thoughts to shampooing her hair and soaping her "reasonably fit for her age" body. As she did every time she showered, she soaped her breasts, moving her fingers in small smooth circles from one breast to the other, checking for any irregularities, a practice formed from losing her mother too soon to breast cancer five years before. With all necessities done, Alison thought it probably wasn't a good idea to linger long in a steam-filled cubical after what had just happened, but she felt fine, though, and she shrugged the whole thing off as her mind drifted to the coming evening with Rich and Tanya.

Tanya was younger than she was, only twenty-nine years old and with a much curvier body. With her buxom hips and fuller breasts, she reminded Alison a bit of Jessica Rabbit, only with long dark hair, unlike the fire-haired cartoon character. She dressed quite hot too, in short or tight outfits. Alison wasn't jealous at all – Tanya was very nice as a friend – but she had noticed a few times John's change in attitude when Tanya was around. Although it wasn't disrespectful, his eyes gave him away, lighting up as she moved in a way that strained the material of her dress, whether it was just an innocent bending over or reaching for a drink or something.

Rich had worked with John for many years. He was older and

had been married years ago to a true nightmare of a woman who'd eventually walked out on him after lots of affairs, which had humiliated him and brought him to the verge of suicide. He'd been treated for depression, which had gone on for about a year, but then everything had changed. He'd booked a holiday in Mexico and met Tanya, who apparently was there with a friend and on her holiday also. Straight away, after returning, he hadn't been able to stop talking about her, and they'd stayed in touch, chatting non-stop.

John and Alison had had many chats about Tanya, worried that Rich might have gone for her on the rebound, so to speak. The way he'd been showering her with gifts and more holidays, they'd questioned whether she was a bit of a gold digger, as Rich was very well off and the ideal target for that sort of advantage to be taken of him. However, Alison, having knowing Tanya now for nearly two years, was sure she would have seen through Tanya's facade and established her ulterior motives by now if there'd been any. On his fortieth birthday, Rich had whisked her away to Mexico and then to Las Vegas, where they'd gotten married, and since then, they'd looked and behaved as if she had made him a very happy guy.

John called from the bedroom, "Hey, babe, all okay?"

She quickly shouted back, "Yep. Fine. You can carry on down if you are ready and fix me a drink. I'm getting out now." After drying herself off, she started getting ready for the evening, and nearly an hour later, she was done. Dressed up in one of her favourite outfits, a snug blue dress, she wasn't competing with Tanya, but with John's eye starting to wander, there was no way that she wanted his eye to come back to a dull-looking wife. And she was far from that in this dress! Still, if she were being honest, Tanya had been great and had never shown any interest in John. Tanya had supported Alison over the last year, and she and Rich looked totally in love.

Her blue dress clinging to her figure, Alison descended the stairs feeling great. John met her at the entrance of the kitchen with a glass of wine, kissed her cheek, and said, "Wow! You look stunning, darling."

She smiled, looked at him as he handed her the glass, said thank you, and kissed him back carefully, not wanting to spoil her lipstick. She was also thinking; *I hope he keeps his interest up for later.*

Their guests arrived finally around 7:30 pm, and as expected, Tanya rocked up in a bright red, tight outfit, and all Alison could think of was the film *The Matrix*. She was sure John was thinking something similar. Rich, same as John, was dressed in smart but casual attire. They both had on polo shirts, John's dark blue and Rich's white, which didn't flatter his slight love handles, Alison thought. They split up, as usual, girls and boys, John dragging Rich off through the rear kitchen door to his magazines, which were out in his garage, and Tanya joining Alison in the kitchen, each clutching their wine. Pretty soon, the evening had been planned out by the girls; they'd decided to ring for pizzas as soon as the guys returned from the garage.

The decision had been made after a couple of glasses of wine and a shuffle of menus they had lying around, and with the wine talking, the girls remembered that a gorgeous-looking young delivery lad called Stuart had delivered the last time they'd had pizza. Then, like a couple of giggling schoolgirls, they hatched a plan, blurting it to the guys as soon as they walked back into the kitchen.

They bet their other halves they could make the poor lad blush when he delivered the pizzas, and if they didn't manage to make him go red or stammer, they would agree to be silent for half an hour while reading one of John's magazines. There was lots of banter and giggling in the next thirty minutes or so and, of course, more to drink, but eventually, the doorbell rang. The girls leapt up, running as best they could in their high heels to the door, giggling and shushing each other. The guys moved a little closer too, but to the side so that they could hear while staying out of the line of sight of the door, just as the doorbell rang for the second time.

Tanya and Alison, trying hard not to laugh, whipped open the door after straightening their dresses and pushing up their breasts to make their cleavages as prominent as possible. Alison started by saying, "Hello. Wow, that was quick; I hope you're not always that quick?" Tanya joined in too with, "Is it hot? I like it hot." After a pause, she added, "Hot but moist in the middle." The lad smiled, blushed, and hesitated, asking for the money and holding out the receipt as Alison swapped it for a couple of notes. Alison said, "Keep the change. It includes a BIG... FAT... TIP...!" ensuring each word dripped from her mouth. The words lingered on her lips as her tongue flicked between them, and it was all delivered with a Marilyn Monroe sultry look — well, that's how she hoped it looked.

Stuart, the pizza lad, stood there open mouthed for a second or two that seemed like an age. Then he broke the tension with an, "Umm, yes, oh, thank you very much," turned on his heels, and bolted in a fluster for his moped waiting at the end of the drive. Barely had the door closed before Tanya and Alison were almost falling over with a fit of the giggles. John and Rich laughed, and Rich said, "The poor lad, he looked like a rabbit caught in headlights. Shame on you two," as he pretended to tell them off. The pizzas were almost going cold by the time they stopped laughing.

Going over every bit of it, mimicking each other's parts in the mischievous joke, Tanya said, "I'm sure he ran at the end because he had a bit of a bulge going on there," setting them all laughing once again. Rich added, "If he crashes his scooter now, ladies, that's going to be your fault!" and John chimed in with, "I wonder what he will say if he is stopped by the law as he swerves about, trying to hide his 'concealed weapon.'" It turned out to be the injection the evening needed to make it a good one.

About midnight, Tanya and Rich said their goodbyes, and, leaving their car there, headed home in a taxi, the plan being one of them would pop by later the next day to collect it. Alison and John had a very brief tidy up and then headed upstairs for bed. Although the drinks had flowed, Alison was probably the worst for wear, flopping into bed, pulling at her clothes, and then turning and almost falling over onto John, who sat on the bed kicking off his socks after pulling his shirt over his head and discarding it on the floor.

As Alison fell onto him, she kissed him on his cheek. Then she traced her lips around to his ear and neck, whispering, "You didn't mind me playing earlier, did you? Teasing that pizza guy? It was just a little fun." Her hand descended to his lap, which was still dressed, but she soon found her mark or, more accurately, the bulge in the trousers. Alison gently caressed the outline as her whisperings on his ear and neck found themselves replaced with her hot tongue flicking. Soon, her teeth joined in, very gently pinching his earlobe, and her hot breath floated in his ear.

He replied, "It wasn't a problem, darling. We encouraged you two. It was a great laugh." The drink had loosened Alison's tongue in more ways than one, and she continued, slurring slightly, "Okay, now I've had pizza. Where is my meat feast?" She tugged at John's zip, and then her hand darted into the open trousers, as did her tongue into his ear and then, as John couldn't stand it any longer, into his mouth, dancing and fencing with his tongue.

Once released, John's hard shaft stood proud from his trousers and encouraged an eager Alison to drop off the bed onto her knees and, while looking up at him, to take him in her hot, impatient mouth. Relaxed by the evening's alcohol, she took him deep, deep down her throat, her hands joining her mouth like it was a team effort, massaging and stroking him until, before long, as she looked him straight in the eye, his balls tightened. She pushed down, holding him as deep as she could without gagging as the hot juice hit and slid down her very willing throat. John's sighs and grunts as he surrendered willingly also told her he was not only spent, but content.

Alison got up. She was also content to have taken the lead and gotten him to relent to sex. Even though she hadn't gotten release herself, it showed she still had it. She could have him, and he wanted her. "Next time, it's my turn, and you can sort me out!" she demanded, as she felt empowered, but John was already asleep where he had fallen back on the bed. Alison swung his limp legs around and onto the bed, finished undressing, and slipped in next to him. She fell quickly asleep, smiling like the cat that had gotten the cream. *Oh yeah, that's right*, she thought as she snuggled into the pillow. *I just did.*

John was awake first in the morning, as he'd planned to set off ten to fifteen minutes earlier than usual to pick up Rich up on the way to work after he had left his car the night before. As quickly as possible, he was showered and dressed smartly in his suit. He kissed Alison on the cheek as she dozed, and then he was away, grabbing a breakfast bar from a packet in the kitchen, jumping into the car, and munching away as he drove. After picking up Rich, they sped into work, with Rich paying for the parking as an appreciation for the lift. John worked in the same building but not the same department, so they walked into the building reception area, did a mutual "see you later", and went their separate ways. John went to the accounts section, while Rich went off to the floors above, to the surveying and architects department, where Rich worked as a technical drawing specialist.

John set to work on an account he had been working on for a while, glancing at the clock as he began. He had started a good forty minutes early, which would help. He called over to his admin assistant, Eva – he wanted to make sure she saw that he was there working early too – and told her that at 10:00 am, he had to nip out to see a client. Eva just nodded and said, "No problem." She would hold the fort.

At around 9:45 am, John got up from his desk, tidied a few papers, and left with a wave to Eva, saying, "I won't be too long, about an hour or so, I should think." As he drove off, he looked again at his watch; it was 9:50 am. Good, he thought. Alison would be at work at the local college, usually 9:15 am for a 9:30 am start. As he pulled up to his house, so did Tanya in her white BMW. Both looked around before they entered the house, John checking to see if the coast was clear and Tanya following him in as he shouted Alison's name to make sure that she had gone.

Once in the kitchen, Tanya grabbed him, and they kissed passionately. John turned to her, pushed her up against the worktop, and then lifted her on it, desperately pulling at her knickers while unzipping his fly with his other hand. Soon, he was thrusting into her, wrapping his hands around her thighs to hold onto the back of her skirted rear, pulling her onto him, driving even harder, making her slide along the worktop with each effort. With her skirt riding up, her bare buttocks moved along the hard, shiny worktop and returned to him again and again. As she moved, it showed him a glimpse of his hard member before it disappeared past the pale pink knickers. Then he froze as his right hand touched something on the worktop behind her. He instantly knew what it was by the tiny noise it made. The small, silver, heart-shaped charm which, when nudged, made a jingle was normally attached to Alison's car keys. His mind leapt to the logical conclusion: keys still here, car still here...

"Alison is still here! Shit! Shit! Shit!"

"What?" said Tanya, confused. John grabbed the keys and barked at her with an urgent, harsh whisper, "Look! Her car keys. Alison is still here! Fuck!"

"Go into the downstairs toilet. If she is upstairs, I will say you are popping back to get something from Rich's car or something. I don't know. Quick, hide." Tanya ran to the downstairs toilet, and John, with his heart pounding, went up the stairs and, while trying to compose himself as quickly as he could, quietly called out as he entered the bedroom.

Clothes and makeup lay strewed about, but no Alison. He then looked into the shower room, a little puzzled, but there was no sign of her, although the shower room was warm and steamy as if it had only just been used. Back in the bedroom, John stood with his hands on his hips when a phone rang. It was Alison's mobile, which sat on the bedside table. Picking it up, John saw that it said, "Trevor work". John pressed the green "Answer" button and put it to his ear.

"Hello, is Alison there please?" a male voice on the other end asked.

John paused and said, "This is her husband; no, sorry, I don't know where she is."

Trevor's voice said, "She is late, so we were just wondering if you knew if she was coming in today. Her class is now waiting."

"Uhh, umm sorry. I will get Alison to call you back. Sorry."

John replied as he disconnected the phone.

John darted back down the stairs to Tanya and explained that she wasn't upstairs, although her car and mobile were still there, so where the fuck was she? Tanya joined him back upstairs, and together they went all over the house and then over it again, looking for her, but she wasn't anywhere to be found. Alison had vanished.

Chapter 3

Julie Pendleton woke up. It was Saturday, but more importantly, it was her tenth birthday. It was barely light outside, and she fidgeted about in her bed, pulling up the quilt with the pop group One Direction printed on it. Then she kicked it back off again, grabbed a book from her bookshelf, and popped back to bed. In no time at all, though, she was bored again. *Why isn't it time to get up?* she thought. Finally, it was time. Well, near enough.

Her mum, Sandra, was the first that day to call out, "Happy birthday, darling!" followed by a big hug and a kiss. Then came her dad, Clive, with another hug and kiss. Clive broke the "love-in" with, "I suppose you had better go and get your prezzies then," and with that, they held her hand and guided her into their bedroom, where they had some presents wrapped up in colourful paper waiting to be torn to shreds.

Julie skipped over the last few feet to the bed, where the presents were sitting ready, and ripped into the parcels quickly: leggings, tops, books, a bracelet, and then finally one that wasn't very big. When she opened the last one, though, her face lit up. "A phone!" she yelled excitedly. "Just what I wanted, Mummy!"

Her dad quickly declared, "Well, we feel you are old enough to be sensible with one, and we know some of your friends have got phones too, so we are putting our trust in you, okay?"

Julie's face was beaming. "Thank you, Daddy. I will be so careful. Honest."

Sandra said, "Okay, hunny, breakfast now, so wash and brush your teeth, young lady, and I will set it all up for you."

"Yes, Mummy," was the reply as Julie flew off into the bathroom to get ready for her big day. Her mum and dad smiled, pleased that the presents, particularly the phone, had gone down so well and that the hot summer day had started as they'd meant it to on their little girl's birthday.

Julie washed and came back into her bedroom to get dressed, trying on this and that, changing her mind and swapping again. "All preparation for when she grows older," Clive joked, and Sandra glared at him for the comment.

As she changed, Julia looked at herself in the full-length mirror her mum and dad had purchased off of eBay for only £20. They had popped down to the village of Hamilton, not that far away, to collect it from a newlywed couple called Tanya and John Fisher. There was nothing wrong with the mirror, but it brought up bad memories for the couple, who had clarified by telling Sandra and Clive that, years ago, John's first wife had bought the mirror at an auction and then, the next day, had simply run off or something and had now been missing for some eight years. He had re-married a friend, Tanya, and now they were redecorating their home, and though he said they would never forget his first wife, it was time to move on. It felt a bit strange, but ah, well, Sandra and Clive didn't need to worry; it wasn't their business. The elegant but plain mirror was in good condition – and cheap – so they'd loaded it into their car and driven back to Winchester before the Fishers could change their minds. That had been the other week, and now Julie was finally using it correctly, and with her new clothes, she could see what she looked like as she pranced around like a little princess.

At midday, they all jumped into the car and headed for the nearest burger joint, where Sandra and Clive paid for the obligatory party of ten screaming kids from her school, including all they could eat and little bits and pieces of goodies. It was the staff's job to entertain the kids so that the adults could sit back and watch them have fun. Also, once all over, it was the staff's problem to tidy up. It all went well, Julie's little friends got her some lovely gifts, and some of the parents who had stayed behind also got a bite to eat and coffee as they all enjoyed the games.

Two of the children, Charlie and Stephanie, got into a bit of a fight when Charlie punched the little girl, and all hell broke out until Charlie's mum grabbed him and smacked his leg. He was ordered to apologise to the now-sobbing Stephanie, whose own mum was very cross and looking like she didn't want to accept the boy's grumpy "sorry" either. However, Sandra just about managed to keep the peace, passing it all off as "too much excitement" and hurrying up the desserts to change the subject and, of course, the atmosphere.

Soon, all had calmed down, and party time was over, with mums and dads collecting their children at around 2:30 pm. Julie had had a very good time, and she asked if her friend Emily could come back for the rest of the afternoon. Sandra didn't mind, but she checked with Emily's parents first, Matt and Kate, who were friendly people and who said yes straight away, deciding to pop back with them for a chat and a cuppa.

It was now past 3:00 pm, and Julie, Sandra, and Clive stood at the door of the burger joint saying their thanks and goodbyes, secretly eager to get back for a cup of tea and a break from so much noise and mayhem. Emily and her parents popping around weren't a problem; it was nice for Julie to have a friend around, but also good to have some adult company while the children played.

They didn't live that far away from the noisy burger joint and were home quickly, with the kettle filled and on in seconds. Excited to show her friend all her new presents, Julie scampered up the stairs with Emily while Sandra piled up all her gifts on the dining room table. Then she decided to call the two girls back down again to collect the presents so that the parents would have some room for their cuppas. As the two girls went back upstairs with full arms, Sandra asked the impossible: "Girls, please don't make too much noise and mess, or you will have to clear it up and come back down here!" Then peace reigned while the cuppas, biscuits, and chat kept the adults busy.

The girls' parents relaxed around the dining table, chatting about holidays, work, and Linda Arnold, who, according to Sandra and Kate, was the talk of the playground because she'd turned up with a new fella while her husband Gordon was "away" on business. True to form, a few of the other mums had noticed the fact that every time he was away, sometimes for several weeks at a time, Linda seemed to be in the company of a new "friend". Also noted was the fact she dressed differently, including make-up, drowning in perfume, high heels, the lot.

They felt sorry for Gordon, but at the same time, as Clive had said, "I bet you women have all kept quiet and not told Gordon either."

Sandra replied, "No. I wouldn't dare!"

Kate agreed, "What if we were wrong?"

Matt laughed. "Hmm, well then, you shouldn't gossip, then, you pair of old hags. You're like old curtain twitchers," he carried on, tongue in cheek, rebuking them but, like most people would be, a little interested in what was going on too.

Sandra's mobile went off, so she picked it up. She listened for a moment and then laughed a little, saying, "Okay, but that's not what the phone is for. Stop messing about." She chuckled, explaining to Emily's parents that Julie had a mobile now. "We did the same as you and got a pay-as-you-go one from town."

Kate nodded her head. "I suppose it's that sort of time to let them start with one. Emily has been good with hers, just playing some games but keeping it off during school lessons, and it has come in handy already. Matt was picking her up from school last Tuesday after coming back from London, but there had been a serious accident on the M3, and the traffic had piled up, so he texted her as he sat in a queue just to say he could be a few minutes late so don't panic. When she finished her last class and switched on the phone, she realised her dad could be a bit late, so she told Miss Price, her math teacher, who walked her up to reception and waited with her until Matt collected her. It was brill! Everyone knew what was going on, the teachers, Emily, Matt, everyone, and best of all, me. Before, I would have been at work and gotten a call, either from the school saying, 'We have a worried child here waiting to be collected,' or a frantic call from Matt saying, 'I'm going to be late; can you call the school?' Now that she can be contacted, I don't have to worry so much."

"Yes, it will be so much better," Sandra said thoughtfully, and of course, she could use it as a little lesson for how the phone should be used and not just for games!

The conversation and cuppa progressed along nicely until the inevitable disturbance arrived. Emily came down the stairs with a petulant face on, and Kate looked around from her seat and said, "What's up, grumpy?"

"It's Julie. She won't play with me anymore," Emily responded.

"Well," said Sandra, acting as peacekeeper yet again, "You tell her that Mummy said she should share her things with you even if it is her birthday, okay?"

Kate joined in encouragingly, "Go on, babe, go on up now. We will be going in a bit, so you haven't got that long left, so play nicely."

Emily reluctantly, slowly climbed the stairs. Then she stopped after a few steps and said, "But Mum, what if I can't find her?"

Kate snapped, "Go and find her! She is only playing. Stop being a ninnie, or you can go home right now!" Emily stomped up the remaining steps, clearly not a happy bunny.

Matt sighed. "Ah, well. We will get going I think, if you don't mind."

"No problem," replied Sandra. "Did you want some cake to take with you?" She quickly cut some pieces of cake and wrapped them in a serviette. Kate said sorry, but Sandra reassured her that it wasn't a problem and thanked her again for popping around. "The trainers you got for Julie's present are ideal." Emily's parents finished up their cuppas, and then Clive quickly showed Matt a couple of bits of DIY he had completed in the lounge while Sandra showed Kate an article in this week's magazine about a cake to make. Again, they were disturbed by Emily coming down the stairs, this time in tears.

"Now what!" said Kate in a huff.

"It's Julie. She won't play."

Sandra, trying to head off the poor little girl's crying from getting any worse, shouted up the stairs, "Julie!" No reply. "Julie! What are you doing up there?" Still nothing. "Emily, what's Julie doing up there?" Sandra asked.

Emily, with tears rolling down her cheek and dropping onto her favourite dress, said, "She's gone. I can't find her."

Sandra was now getting a bit cross too. "JULIE!" she shouted, louder. "ANSWER ME! Now, birthday or not, you will be in trouble in a minute, young lady! Come and say thank you for your trainers – oh, and pop them on to see if they fit okay – and say goodbye to Emily, please. She is about to go home."

There was silence...

Sandra was now getting concerned and quickly headed up the stairs. Clothes and keys were strewn on the floor, abandoned where they had fallen with birthday gifts left untouched. She looked about, but no Julie.

Sandra called out again, getting more cross and then concerned. "Where are you? Come on out, NOW!" She quickly looked about in the landing cupboard with all the towels, then the wardrobes, under the beds, then into her own bedroom, and even into the spare room, which was very sparse, so nowhere to hide in there. Where on earth was she? Then Sandra noticed Julie's new mobile phone on the floor in front of the new full-length mirror. It was still switched on, although the screen the screen was dark, which meant it hadn't been used or played with for a few minutes. She called down to the others, a little panic setting in, "I can't find her!"

They all searched the house, garden, and then the surrounding street, with Emily crying and not making much sense at all, probably thinking, in some way, it was her fault. The adults were getting frustrated at her responses after they'd asked her a barrage of questions when Clive said, "Look, it's no good. She just isn't here, and we are going around and around in circles! We're going to have to call the police, and Christ knows what they're going to think, but we desperately need help." A few minutes later, as the police car's blue lights rebounded off the street houses, the neighbours stood at their windows and doors to see what was wrong while the party balloons bounced around the door of number 12 Cecil Close.

It was normally a quiet little close, with all seven houses occupied by professional-type families that typically kept busy during the week with work or school. You might, on the weekend, occasionally hear the hum of electric mowers grooming the long lawns, but that was as noisy as it got. But not today. Peace was shattered, firstly by a police car, then a police van, then two more cars, then more cars, plain this time, with police detectives. The neighbourhood was completely blanketed with police and other professionals within the hour. The local radio station put out announcements, and parents received text messages to look for a missing ten-year-old child, while the press and TV crews moved in and set up shop. There was absolute bedlam, but there was no sign of little Julie Pendleton.

Detective Inspector James Turner arrived at this manic scene later that day. Quietly at first, he moved around the house, not talking to anyone, listening and absorbing every comment as he went past both the parents and the police officers sitting with them.

A police officer sat with little Emily and her mum, Kate. The little girl, traumatised by the events, was being held tightly on her lap by her mum, who was desperate to protect her from anyone and everyone there, or from whatever or whoever had taken her friend Julie. In the living room, Sandra, also distraught, was talking to a police officer while Clive stood behind the sofa that Sandra and the police officer were sitting on, holding her shoulder to show support.

Emily's dad, Matt, was also comforting his wife and daughter in the other room while the police asked Kate and Emily some of their questions.

Jim Turner acted as he had at other scenes before: he stood quietly, taking in the whole atmosphere of the house, the people in it, the manner of their questions and answers, every part of the scene that he would soon be investigating. He was waiting for something to click or jump out at him, a comment, a fact, or tone of something being said. He wanted everyone there to speak freely to his colleagues until he was ready to ask his questions. The fifty-year-old, slightly greying, slim, suited detective waited, eventually going upstairs to see where the child had allegedly disappeared from. He made notes while passing the staircase, and made a note of the landing window: its high latch was closed, and the small lock of the mid-window latch was inset into the handle.

The stairs and landing were carpeted in a light colour which, he added in brackets, would show up any marks or stains. At the top of the stairs was the parents' bedroom, which was situated to the left of the start of the landing. Then came the spare room or box room. Carrying on, along the left of the landing to the corner came a child's room, with a large bathroom placed on the right. The bathroom door, which had a small frosted glass window, he noted, opened to reveal a luxury toilet, sink, and bath, which was curved at one end and with a glass screen that also curved. *All indications*, he thought, *of a family on a middle-income. The clean and tidy type.*

The box room was very sparse and tidy, with a small single bed with a window above it, this one reachable for a child standing on the bed. *Hmm, a ten-year-old… What height was she? Four to five feet high, perhaps? So, perhaps, easy to reach*, he pondered while looking out. Down below, though, he could see a sheer drop to the paved driveway below. In the child's room, colleagues were busy photographing the layout of furniture, toys, and clothing. *Some brand new, perhaps?* the detective thought, remembering that it was the girl's birthday. All the signs so far were of a looked-after child.

He turned on his heels, made his way back downstairs, and went straight to the mother and the child talking to his colleagues.

He said, "Hello, my name is James Turner, Detective Inspector James Turner. I know this has been a very scary, horrible few hours, but the first few hours are vital in finding young Julie safe and well. I will only be asking a few questions at the moment, as I just want to get a few things clear in my head. Then I think, Emily," he turned his head, addressing directly the small girl clinging to her mum, "you and your mum should go home. It's getting late for a little girl like you." Kate smiled back at the detective, appreciating his sensible approach. "Now then, first of all, please call me Jim. I am here to help find your friend Emily. Your mummy is here too, so don't worry; you're not in trouble, okay?" Emily nodded and tried to smile. "I'm guessing you're a little confused and, of course, worried? Do you think you can tell me, first of all, what you would like to be called by me, young lady? Em or Emily?"

The little girl, almost whispering, replied, "Emily."

"Great, Emily!" answered Jim as he thought, *That's the first hurdle over, getting her to speak to me.* Jim continued, "Now, do you remember my name?"

"Jim," answered Emily.

"Excellent! See, I knew you were a clever girl. So, the first question is really easy. Is Julie taller or smaller than you?"

Silence.

"Okay," Jim continued, "Is Julie the same size as you?"

Emily nodded to confirm, yes, she was the same height. Jim now decided the time was right to press a little more. "Right. When you noticed your friend Julie wasn't in her room, where were you? Were you sitting on the floor or standing up?"

Emily paused and then said simply, "Standing."

"That's brilliant! You're doing so well, Emily. Now, just a few more. If you were standing when Julie disappeared, was Julie sitting on the floor at the end of the bed?"

"Yes," she answered.

"So, Emily, did you see anybody or hear anybody else in the room?"

"No." She started to fidget, getting agitated.

"Okay," he said, backing off a little. "What toy or anything did you last see Julie with?"

Emily, with a moody pout, now said, "Her phone."

Jim pressed on, hoping to get more out of her, as the door of opportunity seemed to be closing on him. "Did she press any buttons and speak to anybody or listen to anyone?"

Silence.

Hmm, thought Jim. *She needs a rest, really, but if Julie is alive, it is so important to get to her quickly.* "Do you remember anything she said?"

Emily thought for a second and then answered in a rush, "She said some numbers as I looked at her new clothes. Then, when I looked around, she had gone!" As Jim took notes, she continued, "I thought she had gone downstairs, so I went downstairs too and told Mummy that Julie didn't want to play with me because she had gone without me. But she wasn't downstairs, so I came back upstairs and looked for Julie, but she was gone, and I didn't know where!" She started crying again, sobbing.

Jim patted her mum's hand and said, "I'm sorry, Mrs

Richards. I will ask you and your husband some more questions tomorrow, but for now, I would like you to go with our wonderful WPC here and go home and get some rest."

He then went through to the other room to Sandra, Clive, and Matt, who were still waiting, chatting with constables and detectives. "Matt Richards?" Jim looked him in the eye, gauging his reaction.

"Yes?" Matt answered straight away.

"Can I just ask you, did you stay downstairs at all times before the young girl's disappearance?"

"Yes," Matt replied as Julie's parents, Clive and Sandra, nodded to confirm his answer to be true.

"When did you first go upstairs?"

"Umm, the same time as Clive, Sandra, and Kate. We all went up after the alarm was raised, and I think I was the last to go up, but I was only within a few steps of them as we all scaled the stairs."

"Okay," said Jim, "would you please go into the other room. You and your family can go home now. There will be a WPC to accompany you all, and please, if there's anything that comes to mind, just tell her, and she can contact me. We will probably need to chat again, I'm afraid, and your car will have to remain here for the time being. The WPC will drive you all home."

Once out of the way, Jim turned to Sandra and Clive. "Sandra, I'm Detective Inspector James Turner. You can call me Jim, and can you just help me a little with a few details? When you went into Julie's room, did you see or hear anything at all, anything strange?"

Sandra shook her head as she sobbed and uttered, "No."

"The phone was on the floor, yes?"

"Yes," Sandra confirmed

"Apart from yourself, was anyone else upstairs to your knowledge?"

"No, just me. Then all the others came to look with me. Clive, Matt, Kate, and even Emily, we were all upstairs looking after I called them up. Until I called everyone up, we were all downstairs having a cup of tea, so we would have seen any strangers or one of us or even Julie come down the stairs or go up the stairs. And because we had been out at the party, all the doors and windows were still locked. There was no other way for Julie or anyone else to get downstairs without going past us, and even then, the only way to go outside is the front door, which we unlocked when we got in from the birthday party. One of your officers has just checked, and the keys are still there, hanging up in the kitchen." She pointed at the pine fixture near the back door with a row of hooks and a few bunches of keys dangling from it.

"What about the back door? Is that locked?" Jim asked.

"Yes," she said, "and it was still locked up until everyone coming looking. We all came in the front of the house, so there was no need to open the back door. The key on the left is the back door key."

He asked his officers who had checked the back door, and then he asked if it was still locked. An officer walked over, tried the door handle, and confirmed it was in fact still locked. Jim went back upstairs again to look at the windows, and all had slight dust and grime on them, which made them look undisturbed. They hadn't been opened recently and were also still locked. Jim had also spoken to a couple of the officers who were first on the scene. He had asked about some of the family backgrounds, but there didn't seem to be any domestic issues like ex-partners or bunny-boiler types, and there were no known problems with social services or rowdy behaviour or even general things like burglaries and incidences of trespassing reported in the area. There just had been nothing reported of any significance. *This will take time to unravel,* he thought, *but do we have enough of it?*

Chapter 4

A few chaotic days went by, with the local and national media coverage hotly active and accusations flying about, as is usual when people aren't aware of all the facts. Jim felt he knew most of the facts, but it was still a mystery, and the pressure was intense. It had been established, with all sorts of alibis, that the little girl had not come down the stairs, and the other girl had been with her at least moments before her disappearance. There was no doubt that access had been limited to the stairs, plus all the windows had been locked and both families had been within sight of the bottom of the stairs. Officers had searched the loft, but it wasn't accessible for the child; there was no way she could have reached it, just like the windows.

The focus would have been on the adults, but they, according to their stories, had been sitting together, chatting the entire time, and they'd confirmed each other's positions both before and after the girl had going missing. Jim had worked hard, trying every angle of questioning. By now, he should have had, and usually would have had, at least a suspicion of an area to follow up, but this one didn't seem to want to conform to the norm. He would have to rely, perhaps, on the forensics, but the reports would take time, and he had hoped for some immediate clues. Jessica Lindon and her team, though, were still working, tidying up loose ends. She had given Jim virtually nothing so far to go on. There was no sign of struggle, no blood, sweat, or tears. Jim had hoped for even a tiny clue to get his teeth into, but sadly, though, there was nothing that didn't seem to fit. It was so disappointing.

The next day, the report landed. Although a couple of the tests were still outstanding, Jim looked through it in sheer desperation. His team, which now amounted to five in number – three male detectives and two females – and colleagues he had worked with before also trawled through the report. Despite the many years of experience between them, they had to admit that they had never been so stumped. There was very little to go on. The two female officers had pretty much lived with Julie's parents in the last couple of days, and if the parents had been hiding anything, the view was that they were bloody good at it because they hadn't put a foot wrong. No one thing or person seemed to be standing out, and they appeared to be upstanding people. Try as he – and everyone else – might, this view was unshakable.

It was Thursday, which meant some three days had passed since Julie had gone missing. The door-to-door enquiries had turned up nothing, not even any gossip, and being a small and quiet close, there weren't even a lot of properties to search and question. By the time late afternoon arrived, Jim had to get out of the office, so he grabbed some reports and headed for his car and home. He didn't live that many miles from the station and was soon pulling up into his driveway. He lived in a simple style of house, a three bedroom semi-detached with a low-maintenance garden consisting of a small flowerbed and a round, paved frontage.

Single for the last five years after his divorce, Jim had tried to make the effort to stay in touch with his ex-wife for the sake of his daughter, Annabelle. She was a similar age to Julie Pendleton, which made it easy for him to imagine the missing child being his own and how he would feel, although that is never truly imaginable for any parent. It all weighed heavily on his mind as he tried to avoid thinking of his own life decisions and their merits.

Dropping his work stuff off in the living room, he went for a shower. Upstairs, he pulled his clothes off quickly, discarding them onto the floor as he went from his bedroom to the shower. Switching it on, it burst into life and soon reached a scalding temperature. Once under the flow, he let the hot water run over his neck and shoulders, instantly relieving some of the tension that had built up during his day at work.

He was still thinking all the time, and he hoped that while showering, a stray thought might pop up, like when you try and remember an actor's name or a song title and, no matter how hard you try, it won't come to you, but then it seems to come to you as you do another task or just relax. *Hmm. Nope, nothing yet.* Shaving as he showered, he wiped the shower glass of the condensation that had been built up by the steam and peered through to the wall mirror, as he had done hundreds of times before.

Switching off for a minute from work, he would now be clean shaven to go out for the evening. Soon, he was done, and he exited the cubicle, dressing in just a T-shirt and jeans. He then quickly made his way out of the house, heading for his favourite little cafe on the outskirts of town. He knew they would give him a quiet corner, which they did, showing him straight to his usual spot.

Then he was seated in comfort, with some paperwork to read through, but to relax properly, he started off with a well-earned pint. He scanned the menu, which he could probably have recited off by heart, and chose the safe option: the roast dinner.

He picked up the forensic report, deciding to study each page and then let his mind wander on the facts and information he had just read.

At that point, his starter arrived, the soup of the day, tomato and beef, with a large chunk of fresh, homemade bread.

He sipped away at the spoonful of soup as he read on, and that was when he noticed something tiny. He decided it probably was nothing, but nevertheless, he got his notebook and jotted it down as a reminder to himself to get it followed up.

In the report, it simply stated that in front of the mirror — this was also cross-referenced with the still photo — there was one trainer sock, white, used (grubby), and no mention of the other second sock to make the pair.

He was now deep in thought as he finished his soup, staring into the empty bowl.

Julie had disappeared with her new trainers on and possibly the socks as well; he frowned at his self-questioning. Her mum, Sandra, had said the room was tidy, with nothing on the floor before they had returned home, so where did the one odd grubby sock come from? It was also next to the mobile phone, which probably, from what Emily had said, was the last thing Julie had touched. If she had been playing with her friend, why would she have had a grubby odd sock on display? With his soup finished, he sat back, his mind chewing on the detail of the report. Was this detail the small point he'd been waiting to jump out at him?

By the time his roast beef and Yorkshire pudding had come out, his paperwork was all over the table, and he had to apologise to the cute young waitress, Chloe. "Sorry, I will clear you a space."

Chloe smiled and put down the plate, which she held with a cloth. "Careful with the plate; it is very hot. is there anything else I can get you, sir? Any sauces?"

James just said, "A drop of English mustard, please," and started to put pepper on his meal.

As Chloe returned with the mustard, he looked at the white cloth draped over her non-serving forearm, where there was a small gravy stain from delivering his food. After she left, his mind slowly ticked over the thought of the cloth, and his mind leapt to the thought of the grubby sock. The two seemed to mix in his mind. *What stains were on the sock?* he wondered.

He looked again at the report as he took his first bites of his main meal, but this time, it was the phone that was the main focus. It had been new that day, which made it great evidence, better than most cases. The only numbers stored in the contacts list were from Mum, Dad, and Emily, and the memory only showed one number dialled, which was to her mum. The memory also showed that it had been answered, confirming times and their locations.

There were no texts and no incoming calls, but it noted in the report that Julie had possibly started dialling a number, or something with the digits 37, which were still showing when the screen had timed out. Why a 37? If caught with a thumb or something, surely it would have been digits placed closer together. The three and seven keys were at the top right and bottom left of a keypad, so that could mean they'd been deliberately selected.

They say, "food for thought," but not much else was coming out of the report at him as he finished his meal and his pint of beer. Chloe returned to clear the plates away, asking if he wanted to see the dessert menu. He decided not to have another course but asked for a coffee. As he looked across at another table, at which sat a family consisting of a small boy and girl with what looked like their mum and dad, he thought of his daughter, Annabelle, and, of course, the missing child, Julie; with a big sigh, he tidied up his paperwork.

When the coffee arrived, he took the opportunity to request the bill. Realising he was now staring at the children at the table opposite him, he broke his gaze away, deciding that tomorrow he would ask his team to follow up a few points and revisit the scene again.

As he drove home to his flat, his mind wandered back to his little girl. Looking at the time, it was only 8:30 pm, so when he stopped the car in his driveway, he picked up his phone and sent a message: "Hi it's Dad. Nothing wrong. I know I haven't been in touch for a while but wondered if you're okay? Love you XX."

Guilt and regrets crept into his mind as the cause of the breakup years ago now came to the front of his consciousness. There was no real blame; that would have been silly, as his job had paid the mortgage and put food on the table, but he'd let it take up too much of his personal time. Kirsty, his then wife, had started hating his lack of consideration, which meant that when the first guy – in the shape of Tom Green – had shown her any attention, the inevitable had happened. Although Jim hadn't been this calm and philosophical at the time, he could now see that the breakup hadn't hurt Annabelle too much, at least he thought and very much hoped that it hadn't.

At fifty years old, he had made the decision that he didn't want to re-marry, as, yes, he was probably mostly to blame for the divorce, having neglected his wife and child. He decided he wasn't going to do that again to anyone else, and to be honest, he couldn't see himself with a different wife other than the one he had lost.

The phone bleeped at him; it was Anna in text speak: "no probs dad it's your bad, not mine, but I'm ok LV U2xxx."

Jim smiled. *I needed that*, he thought as he got out of his car and entered his house. Once indoors, he poured himself a drink, a rum and coke, and slipped off his shoes. The rest of his clothes came off as he climbed the stairs, leaving just his boxers on, and he grabbed the book he had been reading, *Insomnia* by Stephen King, and sat in bed, waiting to feel tired as he relaxed.

Jessica Lyndon got into work at the usual 9:00 am; the office phone was already ringing off the hook. Switching on the light, she dived across the desk to pick it up. "Hi, Jim. All okay?" She had come to know Jim well over the years, mainly when the big cases caused their paths to cross, and if he was phoning at this time of the morning, eager to tell her something or ask a question, it excited her. She had already been draughted in to help with yesterday's missing girl case, so she guessed the call from Jim was in relation to that. She also knew that Jim was heading up the case, which meant that although most of the pressure to find answers would be on him and his team, it would also filter towards other departments, like hers, if they didn't pull their weight.

She listened to him speak and then answered, "Yes, yes, okay. I will get back to you." Her team was starting to turn up, chatting as they arrived, but stopping as they saw Jessica talking on the phone in a serious tone. Once off the phone, she looked at the three of them: Sarah Wilson and Josh Slater, who had both been a part of her team for a couple of years, and Kim Lee, a Chinese student on loan to their department.

Jessica said, "Sorry, guys, but it's the missing girl case, Julie Pendleton. We're going to be under pressure on this one to get her found, so I need some leads followed up quickly. Sarah, can you help me, please? I want to go back over the girl's mobile and the sock. Jim Turner was just on to me, and he could be on to a few points. Josh and Kim, can you to pop back over to the scene of the girl's disappearance. There should be a matching sock to the one forensics bagged yesterday; Jim Turner's team is working on why the socks were separated. I also want you two to help Jim's team at the scene where the sock was found, and possibly, if we find the other sock, we need to know what traces could be on it. Also, can you look at where the sock and the phone were in relation to each other on the floor? The phone was left on the carpet in front of the bed. And can you get some samples of the carpet pile in case anything transferred to or from the carpet fibres? And guys, keep in touch in case we need to update you about anything we find here. We may need to exchange information to add clarity to the proceedings."

Jim Turner came into his office that morning like a whirlwind. He had started the day charged up and eager to get on; he knew it, and so did everyone else after about ten seconds. He gathered his team quickly, firing order after order at them. "More background checks! I want to know about anyone who has been near the house in the last month: postman, parcels from eBay, who was at the girls party, and also anyone who has owned or lived in the house, ever! I want to know about anyone who would possibly have any knowledge of the house and its layout. Anyone from the past who could still hold keys to the place. Check phone records, window cleaners, anyone! I want a list of people who would know which was the girl's bedroom, and mind you, don't upset the guys coming over from forensics today; I have asked them to check some specific details this morning. Keep out of their hair, but also, if they need a hand, please give them one. They will probably do their own thing, but we are all working together to find Julie Pendleton. I don't want any 'them and us' shit getting in the way of this!"

Kim Lee climbed into the passenger seat of the saloon car that Josh had pulled around to the laboratory rear door. All the equipment was already on site, previously transported there for them by a contractor in a van. Josh was a large guy, only in his early twenties, same as Kim, but they were as different as Laurel and Hardy. Josh was probably between around sixteen and eighteen stone, a Gothic nerd with his long black hair, a bit of soft, giant type. Kim was totally different: slight of frame, glasses, short hair. He probably weighed the same as Josh's packed lunch.

But they would help each other, as they had before on other work. Lightening the mood a little, Josh joked about having to sniff out a pongy sock, but they knew that when they did arrive, all the seriousness that their work deserved would be given. Almost there, they swapped ideas of what could have happened to the little girl. Their favourite, as far as they could see, was a distraction letting her either run away or be taken.

Keeping that to themselves, though, they were soon at the address and unloading a few bits from the car while being greeted by the police officers guarding the scene.

The van had delivered the rest of their equipment before the forensics team had turned up, and the police officers helped carry some of it into the house to the restricted area. Josh and Kim quickly changed into their specialist clothing as soon as they arrived: overalls, gloves, shoe covers, etc. Then, crossing the line, they knew it would take time, but that was the nature of their work.

Meanwhile, back at the laboratory, Jessica and Sarah Wilton were already hard at work and felt like they were getting some results. There'd been a bit of an early breakthrough: the sock that had been found at the bottom of the bed on the floor next to her mobile phone in front of the mirror had been scrunched up, not rolled or folded, but scrunched, which indicated it had been used or worn recently.

There were small traces of food, probably from the girls' fingers after returning from the child's party; this showed the sock could have been handled and scrunched just before her disappearance. Then Sarah found a cleaning agent present, a slight trace of a type used for cleaning glass which had even glazed the cotton surface part of the grubby sock. They continued their tests with the sock and the mobile phone.

Jessica called the other half of team on the phone, and she got through to Josh and Kim to see where they had gotten to with their observations and tests. In fact, they had made progress too. The other sock of the pair had been located in the laundry basket on the landing, which also opened a new question: why were the two socks separated? The call from Jessica came to Josh, and he relayed the new results to Kim, in particular about the bagged sock having traces of glass cleaner on it. There was now a theory that, perhaps, the sock had been used on the mirror or one of the windows. Jessica asked that Josh and Kim prioritise their time by dusting all the windows and the mirror, and then by checking all the bedrooms for pieces of food from the sock or the missing girl's fingers to help pinpoint which window or mirror she had touched, perhaps prior to her disappearance. This could help work out her movements prior to her disappearance.

Josh decided to take the window on the landing first. Kim went to the girl's bedroom, going for the bedroom window first. Then, he would carry on to the mirror a while later. Soon, Josh had finished the window at the end of the landing, drawing a blank, although slight traces of cleaning agents, dust, and grime were on top of the surface and mixed, showing they hadn't also been touched. There were no traces of food or fingerprints.

Moving out to the parents' bedroom, he walked along the landing and glanced inside the child's room to see Kim standing at the bedroom window, working. Josh continued to the parents room, the main bedroom, and worked away for quite some time. With the larger window in their room, and the mirrors on the wardrobe doors, the testing took some time. Josh, after a while, possibly a couple of hours, decided he, if not Kim, needed a break. He hadn't gotten such a large frame without a large intake of food. Calling down to the officers downstairs by the front door, Jim Turner's team, he asked them if anyone was going for lunch or sticking the kettle on.

The guys downstairs shouted back some abuse, having a laugh and a bit of banter, reminding Josh that his mate Kim hadn't asked for lunch. Drawing a link to this and the difference in their sizes, Josh held his own in the exchange of words, giving back as good as he got. Although it was a serious subject – a missing young girl – it all helped them deal with the shit that could turn some people's heads and minds.

With not a sound coming from Kim, Josh turned and made his way down the landing to the girl's bedroom, where he knew Kim was working. Pausing just before the doorway, he started to throw a derogatory remark Kim's way, but then he froze, his heavy frame now silent as his eyes widened.

Chapter 5

The phone rang in Jessica Linton's office, and although very busy, she broke off to answer it. Sarah looked up, sensing something wasn't right. She couldn't hear the words, but from Jessica's tone, she knew she had to pay attention for a moment not to her work, but to a woman who she could see was shocked! Jessica was older than Sarah's twenty-seven years, but Sarah still had an empathy with her boss, a thirty-seven-year-old, smartly dressed, very professional woman in a professional field, but now Sarah was not looking at her boss but at a woman in need of her support.

Quickly removing her latex gloves and leaving her desk, she moved towards Jessica, who had one hand on her mouth as if she was almost stopping herself from coughing or calling out. The other hand looked like it was about to drop the phone onto its receiver at height. Sarah called from just a few yards away as she rushed to Jessica's aid, "What's happened? What's wrong?"

Jessica turned to her younger colleague. Although Sarah was her junior, Jessica knew she would need her now. She stuttered her reply, "I-i-it's Kim."

Sarah said, "Yes, what did he want?"

"No, it's Kim."

Sarah was confused. "Yes, what about him? Who was on the phone?"

"It was Josh on the phone. I can't believe it. Kim has gone."

"Gone?" Sarah repeated, puzzled. "Gone where?"

"I don't know," said Jessica. "He's disappeared, same as the girl."

"What?" said Sarah. "You're not making any sense, Jess? Kim? Has disappeared too?"

"Yes, that was Josh. He said he went to the room where Kim was working, he thinks about forty minutes ago, and it was empty."

"Kim has gone? Gone where? Left the site?"

"No," said Jessica, getting emotional now, "he has disappeared into thin air!"

Jim Turner headed to the house of the missing child in total disbelief. *What on earth are those clowns up to?* he thought.

His team had rung him, telling him someone else had now gone missing. It was so confusing. They said it was the Chinese guy who was part of Jessica's forensic team. *This is in danger of becoming some kind of joke*, he thought as he drove.

Arriving at the scene, he went quickly into the house. Once again, there was bedlam, with his team, the normal plods, and the remaining forensic guy, the big lad he had seen before, all waving their arms about and shouting. It took some time, but after getting the facts, Jim made his way to the room, and looking from the doorway, he peered around. There wasn't much there, for Christ's sake, a chest of drawers, a single bed, a small wardrobe in plain pine, and a free-standing full-length mirror. Apart from that, there was a small TV on the chest of drawers, a few bits set about the room like ornaments, a PlayStation, and some storage under the bed too. *Those are pull-out drawers*, he thought to himself. *Quite tidy for a ten-year-old*.

Shaking his head, he was baffled, but he knew that in no time at all, the pressure would double. A shout from downstairs broke his concentration; it was Jessica and her assistant Sarah. He called down to the officers to let them up. Jessica was straight into him, asking questions; he batted them away as best he could for a minute with the fact that he had only just arrived himself and was unaware of the full picture.

Quickly bringing her up to speed as best he could, he suggested totally sealing off the room again. Something, of course, was very wrong and needed investigating further, but the last thing he needed was anyone else disappearing! It was one thing for a ten-year-old to go missing, but a full grown adult? That would change everything.

Later, most left the house, including Jim, Jessica, and her assistant Sarah, plus a few others, their heads hanging in defeat yet again with nothing to show for their efforts on a day that at first had shown some promise. Jim suggested to Jessica that they meet for a meal later that evening, where they could discuss how to proceed. This would give Jessica time to call Kim's family, but what on earth she could tell them, who knows.

They were to meet in his favourite cafe, and Jim arrived first and waited patiently with a pint. He had said around 8:00 pm, and he could understand Jessica being a little late. His phone lit up and buzzed. It was her. "Sorry, Jim. I'm running a bit behind, but I'm on the way now."

It wasn't too bad, about fifteen minutes, and she came into

the small cafe. Jim sat in the corner, his favourite spot, out of the way. He held his hand up as if it was needed to show her where he was in a "here I am" sort of way, and then he cringed a little at his own awkwardness, his slightly nervous display to a woman that he thought attractive but also more of an equal and who was head of her own department.

Probably what had put him on the back foot was the fact that he found himself looking at her in a different way now. She was a professional woman, and always before, she had conducted herself in that way, dressed in her smart work attire.

But here she was now in a dress which was quite figure-hugging but still elegant, black with tasteful jewellery on show, her hair done differently, but also, her demeanour had changed, perhaps due to her missing employee and, of course, because she was now on her own time. He also thought that a nice cosy café, perhaps a restaurant, would have fitted better, but that would have been a bit too pretentious.

Quickly offering a seat opposite his own, he made that exact point, almost apologising for the location of the meal. Jessica jumped at the apology with, "No, don't be silly. It's not a date or anything. We have stuff to discuss, and it looks a nice, friendly place anyway, Jim. Don't worry, honestly. Please, just relax."

Jim replied, "Okay, thanks. Now, how did you get on telling his family? How bad was it?"

She gave a big sigh and then answered, "Well, I did cheat a bit, what with such a lack of answers and not knowing what the hell is going on. I told them an edited version of the day's events. I said we are a bit confused with Kim leaving work early today and wanted to check if they had a family emergency or anything that had called him away. Then I said how great he was getting on and if he gets in touch with them to give me a call or even get him to give me a call."

Jim agreed with the way she'd handled it, saying, "That's really all you could have done. Just to help me, can you pass on their contact details, if you haven't already done so, to my department, please?"

Jessica answered, "Yes, sure, Jim. No problem. I will email you all I have on Kim tomorrow. Background, contact details, and anything else I feel is relevant. I can give it all to you tomorrow from the office. Is that okay?"

"Yes, that's fine. I've got to ask, Jessica, and please don't take offence, but I need to know. Is there any way Kim would have known Julie Pendleton or her family or have any other connection?"

Jessica wasn't happy with the inference that Kim could have had anything to do with the disappearance of the young girl, but she understood the question had to be asked. The answer was the same as it had been from his family: there seemed to be no connection. Jessica also pointed out that, for starters, he hadn't been in the country or the area for very long.

Questions and answers went on and on until their meals arrived, and they paused from the work-themed meeting and lightened up, asking each other how their families were keeping. Jim also tried to find out if there were any men on the scene in Jessica's life. Jim knew she was a career woman, and he hadn't had a chance to socialise with her before, but the conversation flowed easily, and the indication came back that she was on her own, her only romantic episodes being a few brief encounters.

Jim decided to tackle the tricky subject of questioning her employee Josh, who had been there in the house when Kim had vanished.

Jessica, as he thought she would be, was defensive, but he

made it quite clear it had to be done as soon as possible and that she was, of course, welcome to sit in on the interview.

Jessica backed off a little, realising as a professional that Jim had given her a courtesy, because in no way did he have to extend an invitation to her, but it did sweeten the request sufficiently, keeping a pleasant evening on track.

They decided to meet early the next morning at her office, where they could talk to Josh and not seem too threatening to him. Jessica was thinking of her employee's feelings, but Jim's thought was that he wanted Josh talking freely. He didn't think Josh had caused Kim's disappearance – well, not unless he had eaten him! – but he would know everything that had led up to his partner's disappearing act.

Pressing his luck, Jim then asked Jessica if she would like a drink after the cafe at a bar around the corner. It was walking distance, in fact.

Jessica said, "Thanks, but drink-driving and all that."

Jim quickly jumped in, replying, "No, of course not. Just wondered. I only live down the road. No strings attached, but seeing as we are going to your office in the morning anyway, I have a spare room. Honestly, there is no problem if you would like to stay over. I'm sure it's been a very long day."

Jessica paused before answering. She thought, *Will this be seen in any way wrongly by others?* She had no worries with Jim; he was pleasant company and always treated her as an equal and a professional woman. She said, "Hmm, I will just nip to the ladies before I answer that, if you don't mind."

Really, she was being practical, wondering what was with her in her handbag. Returning a few minutes later, Jessica leaned over, gave Jim a kiss on the cheek, and let him down gently, saying, "Sorry, Jim, maybe another time. As you say, it's been a very long day, and I want to be home tonight."

Jim was very disappointed, but he tried hard not to show it. "No, you're absolutely right. I should not have asked you. Really sorry, that wasn't very professional of me, was it? Especially before all this is sorted. You must be so concerned about Kim and Josh too."

Jessica smiled and said, "It's okay, really. I don't mind the invite. It's just been a long day. Honest. I'd love to have a longer evening another time when my mind wouldn't be elsewhere."

It was dark but not very late when they walked back to their cars. Jim's was a black Audi, and Jessica's a white BMW.

Jessica again thanked Jim for a nice evening, under the circumstances. Jim returned the gesture.

Then, almost like awkward teenagers, they looked at each other again, but this time, their eyes seem to lock together in a fixed gaze, and so did their lips. First of all, they pressed together quickly and lightly. Then, as Jim cradled the back of Jessica's head, his hand slipping under her long hair, their lips met again, but this time, they crashed into each other, opening to allow a full, passionate embrace. When they parted, they both were a little breathless and shocked

Without a word being spoken, they had almost subliminally decided on a passionate embrace, to both their surprise.

Jessica was first to talk. "Right, okay. Umm, well, see you in the morning, then?"

Jim looked equally stunned, replying, "Yes, yes, I will be there around eight am, okay?"

"Sure, okay, Jim. I will see you in the morning. Good night."

Jim called back, "Night," as they jumped into their cars and set off, both with their minds in turmoil. Jim wondered, *Was that a mistake or destiny?*

Chapter 6

Early the next morning, Jim walked into the main forensic lab. It was already open, the light was on, and Jessica, Josh, and Sarah were in the office. Jessica had obviously gotten there a bit before him and no doubt had briefed her remaining staff that he was coming with any new information on this stage of the situation.

Jessica noted his arrival and acknowledged him with a handshake when he came into her office. Sarah got up, leaving the office clear for the others to discuss Kim's disappearance. She tried to smile, and she mumbled a good morning to Jim in passing. It was nothing against him; it was just an emotional time, and she was best serving her colleagues by leaving them to sort the latest developments without her help.

Jim then turned to Josh, extending a hand while saying, "Morning. Josh Slater? I am Detective Inspector Jim Turner." Josh confirmed to Jim that he had addressed him correctly by looking up from his seated position, his unshaven face showing signs of lack of sleep, and mumbling, "Hi." He shook Jim's outstretched hand, obviously feeling concerned and apprehensive.

"Now then, I had a little chat with Jessica, and I don't want you getting too worried about this, but with what's happened, I have to start with yourself. Now, Josh, after a night to think about it, is there anything you would like to add to your initial statement you gave to my colleagues on site yesterday?"

Josh shook his head, screwed up his face, and replied, "I wish I could think of something honest."

"Okay," said Jim. "Let's just chat over some of it, then?" He then continued without waiting for a reply from the young man. "Kim Lee, how did you get on with him?"

Josh answered without hesitation. "Fine, really, no problems, no confrontations, or anything."

Jim said, "He must talk to you. Was there anything he was particularly into?" Josh's face looked quizzical, but Jim clarified by adding, "Gambling, women, porn... What was his hobby or spare time used for?"

Josh was a bit embarrassed, explaining he didn't really talk or socialise like that with him. This was not for any particular reason but because Josh had his own hobbies of thrash metal music and heavy metal friends and was into online gaming, while Kim seemed to keep to himself. "I think he was a family-focused guy who seemed to stay at home studying."

Jim cut in, saying, "A bit of a swot, then, would you say?"

"Yes," replied Josh. "I like to enjoy my spare time, going to festivals, listening to music, sharing it with my mates, and I go to the cinema too nearly every week, but I don't know if Kim went to the cinema or anything. He just seemed a real homely type."

"Right," said Jim. "Tell me more about that day? In your statement, you said you were in the parents' room, inspecting the windows. What was Kim doing?"

Josh answered, "As I said in the statement, I walked by earlier as he had finished the windows in the girl's room. I think he had started then on the free-standing mirror."

"In his abandoned notebook, which was on the floor, there were two numbers. Did you know that?"

"No," said Josh. "What numbers?"

"Yes," said Jim. "Two threes and the number seven, or 337. Any idea why this was written?"

"No idea!" said Josh.

Jessica jumped in at that point, saying, "That's the same sort of numbers that were on the missing girl's phone."

"Yes," said Jim, "but he was looking at the window and the mirror. There was no mobile phone this time." He turned to Josh again and asked, "Did you hear him say anything before his disappearance?"

"Nope, nothing at all," said Josh.

"Okay, Josh, that will do for now. Of course, if you remember anything, tell Jessica or me as soon as possible."

Josh nodded his acceptance without words. He rose from his chair awkwardly, as he was aware that both Jim and his boss, Jessica, were quiet, and he left the office knowing they were waiting for his exit before talking.

Jim looked to Jessica and said, "This number thing is really bugging me! Has Sarah come up with anything from the phone?"

"Not really anything more than what you know already. We have worked out, though, that the number three button was pressed first and then the seven button, but not the green button, which would indicate no phone call was made. It wasn't sent as a text either. The partial fingerprints were unique to Julie Pendleton, so she was the one who pressed the buttons."

"At least when Julie Pendleton disappeared, her friend Emily was in the same room. Surely she saw or heard something? People just don't disappear into thin air!" Jim placed his hand on Jessica's shoulder. "I will do my very best for Kim and the girl. There's got to be a simple answer to this."

Jim left the forensic lab with very little to go on, and as his car started up, he gave a big sigh as he decided to go and chat with Emily Richards and her parents. From the car, he phoned and asked the WPC at the Richards' house to let them know he was on his way and wanted to interview Emily again. Before hanging up, he added, "When you let them know, would you also note their reactions to my imminent arrival?"

Jim was just trying anything he could to rattle or push a sign out of them. The sort of thing he wanted to know was if they panicked a little or if they'd coached their child into saying something, even with a nod or maybe a subtle threatening look.

When he arrived, the WPC whispered that they'd had a normal reaction and just seemed to want to help. They all sat down together in the living room, with the WPC on one side of the room and everyone else on the other. Kate and Matt Richards sat on Emily's left side, and Jim was on her right. Her parents were, of course, very protective of their daughter's feelings, and together, they hugged her reassuringly as she sat between them on the settee.

Jim waited for a moment before cutting to the chase. He really didn't know how long he had left to find Julie and Kim, so unfortunately, if other people's feelings were stepped on, then so be it! Jim knew that, soon, the chief superintendent would be on his back, wanting results. "Hello, Emily," Jim said. "Remember me?"

Emily confirmed with a nodded yes.

"Now, just like last time, I would like to chat with you and your mum and dad. Now, our chat wasn't scary before, was it? So don't worry; we are just going to try and think where Julie might be. It'll be just like a bit of a game, but it's a serious game, okay?"

Emily held onto her mum as she nodded to confirm that she knew what was required of her.

"Firstly, I ask all of you, Mum, Dad, and you, Emily, if you know a Chinese man called Kim Lee at all?" They all looked shocked. They didn't expect to hear that question, and quizzical looks flitted between them all, so Jim pressed on. "Have you seen any strangers at or around your home or at school over the last month? Is there anything unusual that has sprung to mind?" They all shook their heads and muttered quiet nos.

Jim continued, "Emily, when you and Julie were in her bedroom, did anybody at all come into the room before Julie disappeared?"

"No," said Emily.

Jim said, "When I say, did anyone come into the room, I mean even someone you know, not just a stranger."

"No," said Emily again.

"Okay," said Jim, "did anyone shout or whisper anything to you or Julie?"

"No."

"Was Julie holding the phone?"

"Yes."

Jim asked, "As Julie pressed the buttons, did she say anything or speak into the phone?"

Emily looked at her mum and dad and said, "Well..."

Jim's eyes lit up. *Might there be something here?* "Well, what? Anything, however tiny, even if you think it was silly or you think it could get you or Julie into trouble, could be useful."

Again, Emily turned her head, looking for support.

That's it! Jim knew he had caught on to something, but had he hit the jackpot?

He coaxed some more, trying to reassure her, "Look, Emily, your mum and dad are here. You or Julie won't be in trouble at all, I promise. There you go, your mum and dad heard that too, and WPC Wilson has even written it into her little book, so I won't be allowed to change my mind."

Emily looked again for reassurance, and then she said, "Julie saw the numbers in the mirror and put them on the phone."

"Okay," said Jim, excited by at last getting something. "What were the numbers? Can you remember?"

The young girl answered, "Number three and number seven."

"Okay," Jim pressed on, "did Julie say anything?"

"As I looked away, I heard her saying three seven as she pressed the buttons."

"Then what?" asked Jim.

"She was just gone!"

"Were there any other noises? Or did the phone make a noise at all?"

"No," said Emily. "I looked around the room and thought Julie was hiding from me, playing a trick."

Jim's head was spinning, it was so puzzling, but at least there were some clues at last. "Where on the mirror were the numbers? Do you remember? On the wood or the glass?"

She answered, "On the glass, like when Daddy starts the car in the morning."

Jim looked across at Matt Richards, who jumped. Like the others, he had been engrossed in his daughter's account. Then he'd been worried at what his daughter was trying to explain.

Kate stepped in, saying, "Ah, I know. Do you mean when I sometimes write a message to Daddy on the glass screen?"

"Yes," said Emily.

Kate then clarified, saying, "I sometimes write a message to Matt on his windscreen, like say, 'I love you'. Then, when he puts the heater on after starting the car, the message appears like magic the next morning in the condensation."

"So it was like condensation? Misty?" Jim asked the child.

"Yes," said Emily.

"Was it just those two numbers though? Anything with them?"

"No," said Emily. "Just the numbers three and seven."

"Right. That's great. You have been fantastic, Emily. Well done. Kate and Matt, have you any idea what the numbers three and seven, or thirty-seven, what they might mean to you, your daughter, or what they might mean to your friends and their daughter, Julie?"

"No," Matt answered, and Kate added, "We can't think at all."

Jim, now with the bit between his teeth, raced over to the Pendletons, who, because of their house still being sealed off, were staying in temporary accommodations. Clive answered the door, and Jim could see the desperate hope in his eyes. Clive quickly asked, "Any news?"

"No, sorry, Mr Pendleton. I just have some questions to ask that could help find your daughter. If I may?"

Clive invited him into where Sandra sat on the edge of her seat. She looked expectantly at Jim as he walked in. With Jim, again, was WPC Williams; she was there to help. The two sat down next to Sandra, and they reassured her that no news could be good news.

Once everyone was seated and the parents were calm, Jim first asked if they knew a Kim Lee. They said they didn't know him and had not seen any strangers around recently. Jim told them that Kim had also disappeared, to which they showed their concern and puzzlement.

Jim then asked about the mirror. Where had they bought it from? Had they ever seen any numbers appear on it? Confused and puzzled, they answered that they didn't know of any numbers on the mirror and that they had bought it from a couple in a little place not far from the village of Hamilton. Then Clive remembered something. "Hang on a minute." His eyes were wide. "Inspector, when I bought the mirror for £20 off the couple, I'm sure they mentioned something about the husband's first wife being the one who used to own it, but she left, never to return. They said she also just mysteriously vanished! At the time, I took it to mean she'd just run off with someone, but now..."

"Well," Jim said, "it's worth following up, but don't jump to conclusions. There could be nothing in it, but I promise you this, Mr and Mrs Pendleton, I will follow up every lead if it means finding your daughter."

Chapter 7

After leaving the Pendletons', Jim set off for his home. The day had at least yielded clues to this strange mystery, even if there was not yet a sign of the missing.

On his hands-free phone, as he drove, he rang Jessica Linton. He didn't have to, but he felt the forensics could also help with solving the mystery as to where the missing had gone. Plus, of course, he still wondered about the lingering kiss they'd shared last night as they'd parted company. While driving, he explained about the new lead. Jessica agreed to look at the mirror; they would get it collected and brought to the lab the following morning.

Jim agreed that this would be better, and he told her that he would then have his team rip up all the flooring of the house. Even though there wasn't a mark on the carpet to show it had been disturbed, it would be another avenue explored and discounted. Jim didn't push it with Jessica but simply asked how she and her staff were coping with Kim's disappearance. Jessica replied that they were doing okay and trying to focus on finding him.

The phone call ended before Jim got to his house. Jessica

said she was just leaving work. It was 5:30 pm, after all, and it had been another long day.

Jim entered his home, chucked his keys on the kitchen table, and poured a stiff drink, wondering what to do for tea. Then, just as he brought the drink to his lips, his phone rang; it was Jessica again. "Hiya. All okay?" he asked.

She answered, "Yeah, just wondered, if you weren't doing anything tonight for a meal, if you wanted to risk my cooking? I was thinking of doing a spaghetti Bolognese?"

He was surprised and even taken a little aback, but he said, "Great, I'd love to," almost before she had uttered the actual invitation.

"Okay, I will see you around eight pm? I will text you the address."

Well, that's a turn up for the books, he thought as he sprinted upstairs to the bathroom to get himself ready, still holding the drink, which now was at half-mast. It slopped as he guided it along, and he thought, *No more than that one so I'll be able to drive. Plus, you never know...*

Jim drew into Tungsten Green, a modern estate of detached housing with its own green area in the center of the select group of houses. Jim had found the address easily after stopping briefly on the way to get a bottle of wine. Parking wasn't a problem; with Jessica's car already in the driveway, he simply parked across the front of the driveway access.

Even though he had known Jessica for a few years in passing, he was now possibly a little apprehensive or nervous. This wasn't the work situation, or even a neutral territory like the cafe had been.

But, with a deep breath, he adjusted his dark-blue long-sleeved shirt, looked down at his black trousers, and tapped the heels of his smart black shoes together as if he was Dorothy in the Wizard of Oz.

He cleared his throat with a stifled cough, which was more nerves and habit than anything else, just before knocking twice on the red front door with its brass fixings.

Whilst waiting, he managed yet another small cough and a large intake of the night's air before the door was snatched and swirled open. Jessica stood in the doorway, smiling now, more confident in her own home, of course. Straight away, she shouted out a loud, "Hi! Come on in, Jim. Ooh, lovely wine, thank you. That's very nice of you."

Jim mumbled, "It's the least I could do, if you're kind enough to cook."

Jessica offered Jim a glass of his own wine, or would he like to choose from her well-stocked cabinet? Jim accepted the invite of the glass of the red he'd bought, and as Jessica set about finding a corkscrew from the kitchen, Jim took a seat on the white leather settee in the tidy, almost anaemic room.

Very minimalistic, he thought, but he did like that it showed a person confident and together, in charge of her surroundings with things in their place.

Jessica seemed to have a relaxed outfit on, possibly a summer dress, and no footwear. Her jewellery was just a necklace with a solitaire diamond, and her hair was down again – all signs of her being relaxed and confident, which he found attractive.

Returning from the kitchen with two glasses of the red stuff, Jessica handed a glass over to Jim and asked if he had found the place okay. At the same time, she reached behind him, notching up the smooth music a little. Jim clasped the glass in his right hand as she reached behind him and moved the retro stereo unit controls. He didn't quite know where to look, as the top of Jessica's dress slightly cupped open at the edge a couple of inches from his face, exposing her cleavage down to a black and white lacy bra, which showed him her half-cupped, firm-looking breasts.

Jim wasn't sure how he should look away without looking silly, so he resorted to just looking upwards while breathing out a silent "phew". But all that succeeded in doing was to blow the gentlest caress of air teasingly over the soft-skinned area, making her skin tingle.

Jessica pulled back after adjusting volume control, realising she had inadvertently had an effect on Jim's breathing, and her nipples also responded, pushing against the thin layers of material.

Twisting around, she sat back down with a leg crossed under her at the other end of the two-seat settee, facing Jim.

He, in turn, twisted around to an open posture towards Jessica, who he was finding increasingly more attractive and interesting than he ever had in all the years of crossing her path.

Work was sidestepped by both as much as possible, with the conversation lingering only on family and social aspects. Both were desperate not to think for a while about their demanding jobs.

Before long, Jessica jumped up and dashed to the kitchen to dish up their meals.

Jim was pleased that she hadn't overfaced him with the portion size, because, with a glass or two of wine, he could see himself ending up slumped down, especially in such comfy seating and pleasant company. They chattered away, keeping the conversation rolling along with no awkward silences.

Once the meal was finished, Jim helped by taking out the dishes to the kitchen. Jessica opened the dishwasher and quickly placed the dishes into their correct sections so that they would be ready to be washed later. Without stopping, she turned to the freezer section of the fridge and took out two small tubs of ice cream and, once again, sat on the settee with Jim, who looked across at Jessica as she struggled to push the small plastic spoon into the hard, frozen dessert.

Jim suggested warming the spoon in her mouth. Jessica smiled, looked up from her dessert, and put the small spoon in her mouth. Still staring at Jim, with a seductive smirk and trying not to giggle, Jessica removed the spoon from her mouth, a wicked glint in her eye, and then she returned it, now warm, to its task, where it easily cut through the ice cream.

As she lifted it towards her mouth, the warm spoon made the small amount of ice cream very slippery, and it dropped off the spoon and landed on top of her cleavage above her dress top. Upon hitting the bare skin, it instantly started to melt further, making Jessica gasp, "Now, look!"

Jim burst out laughing, but at the same time, he dived across her, quickly shoving his spoon below the sliding ice cream and preventing it from going any lower, either on down into her bra or marking her dress. This was followed by a very innocent, honest attempt to scoop it up, and without thinking, he popped it into his mouth with an "Mmm." That was it; that was the real icebreaker, and both ended up crying with laughter.

Jim reached across, wiping away a tear of laughter from her cheek, and in that moment, the mood instantly changed. Jessica moved her cheek against his strong, warm hand and then kissed it.

Jim moved his other hand behind her head, cradling it as he moved his head in to meet hers. Their lips touched, so gentle at first, then bumping furiously together until they parted to allow their urgent, passionate tongues to take over the offensive now, pushing, probing, and entwining, responding in a way their bodies soon would be.

The remaining ice cream was abandoned to the night, one appetite swapped for another, more intense one. The settee yielded to their movement as Jessica slipped down and Jim assumed the dominant position on top of her, his body slipping between her opening legs, the bottom of her dress automatically rising as she wriggled lower beneath him.

Their mouths remained locked together, but their hands were free to explore; Jessica's hand was at Jim's waistband, pulling at his trouser belt, and Jim's hands were releasing her breasts, extracting them from her bra and dress.

Then, with his thumb and forefinger, he rolled and teased her now very hard nipples, making her gasp.

But she wasn't going to let him have it all is own way; she had fire in her eyes. She had conceded the dominant position, but times had changed, she was a modern woman, and she wanted the hot sex just as much as any man.

Once her hand felt his warm, hard shaft, she tugged it free of his trousers, gripping it. She didn't wait for what Jim wanted to do, but nudging her lace panties to one side, she took him and placed him at the entrance of her moist lips.

Jim tried to thrust forward, but she was having none of it, holding him there. She was now regaining control.

For a fleeting moment, it crossed Jim's mind that there was a problem. Then he looked at her face, her teeth clenched in a determined look, and she hissed, "Not yet." He was a little puzzled, but then he felt her move the head of his urgent, hard shaft over her wet lips and against her firm clit. Jessica was using Jim's cock like a toy, teasing him but also herself, pressing it against her hot, firm bud and rubbing it, using her juices as a delicious lubricant as she worked harder and faster.

Jim moved his head down to her nipples, sucking hard on them, using his teeth as well as his lips, trying to tease her. But as he tried to regain control, Jessica knew exactly what she was doing, rubbing him against herself harder and faster, building her climax. She was going to take her orgasm; it was hers, and she wanted it.

Looking at him with her teeth still clenched, she rubbed frantically as his large, engorged head moved along her lips and over her swollen clit, faster and faster.

Jim's mind had gone now; he had no control at all. His head raised from her breasts, and his mouth was open; he was not sure whether to cry or shout for joy. Jessica started to pant, and then her breathing paused for a moment and then expelled as her body jerked in orgasm.

That triggered his orgasm, and he jetted his hot juices as her grip relaxed on him, enabling him to thrust forward finally, releasing his last few jets while now fully buried inside her.

Jessica and Jim had almost passed out in the final throes of passion, but now it was time for their bodies to reflect on what had just happened between them. Was it just raw need? Or was there a spark of something special between them? But, for now, these questions could wait as they basked in the afterglow and their minds and bodies were as one together as lovers.

Chapter 8

Detectives Trevor Symmons and Simon Hern knocked on the door of a house in the small village of Hamilton. They had been asked to follow up on a mirror that had been bought on eBay from a couple at this address.

They knocked, waited at the door, and eventually, the figure of a woman appeared. "Hello, can I help you?" she asked. The two detectives introduced themselves and asked if her name was Mrs Tanya Fisher. She answered yes, a little puzzled why two detectives were there standing at her doorstep.

She let them inside, where she called for her husband, John; the detectives asked him to confirm that he was John Fisher and then explained that they were following up on a few details about an old mirror that had been bought from them.

John confirmed that they had sold the mirror to a couple some time ago. He asked, "Why, is there a problem?"

Detective Symmons said, "The couple who bought it placed it in their daughter's bedroom, and on her eleventh birthday, the daughter disappeared while she played with a friend."

John's face went white and then grey. Simon picked up on the change of mood, and he also noted that John's and Tanya's gazes darted across at each other. He thought straight away that he had hit a nerve, and he followed up by asking, "Have you something to tell us, Mr Fisher, involving the disappearance, or the mirror, perhaps?"

"Well, yes," said John Fisher. And out came the story of his first wife, Alison, her disappearance, and how he had endured years of suspicion and gossip because of the affair he'd been having with Tanya, who was now his wife. Tanya joined in with the story of how her then-husband, Richard Blake, had heard all the talk and could stand it no more and had committed suicide by taking his car to a lonely spot in the New Forest and attaching a hosepipe to the exhaust, running the car's engine until he was gone. He'd been found eventually by a chap walking his dog.

The detectives were stunned and surprised. "So, let's clarify this. Your first wife, Alison, also disappeared?"

"Yes!"

"Oh my God! Where did you get this mirror from, Mr Fisher?"

John confirmed it was from an auction house and even

fished out the invoice, which stated it was lot 351 sold to a Mr J Fisher for the sum of £50.

The two detectives thanked the couple, and taking the invoice with them, they returned the car, scratching their heads. Then Detective Symmons picked up the phone and called Jim.

Jim Turner was at his desk, looking through paperwork, when he received the call from his detectives, whom he had sent to follow up on the mirror lead. The news that there was, in fact, a third missing person came as a surprise.

Jim called the number from the invoice to talk to the auction house about lot 351. It turned out that the mirror, along with other old furniture, had been received from a house clearance, where, they believed, an old lady had once lived before passing away.

The couple had bought the mirror as described by Mr Fisher, and it had been collected by Mr Fisher and his wife Alison Fisher. Jim took the trouble to check their descriptions and make sure that they matched.

The auction house tried to help as best they could, but all

they had on the previous owner of the mirror before the Fishers, the old lady, was an address. There was no name and no telephone number.

It wasn't long before Jim pulled up in his car to where the satnav had directed him for "the old lady's address". It was at another little village setting in a place called Botley, but there was now some very new looking housing there, or what would be best described as a group of linked properties. He went to work tapping on doors and was disappointed to find out – as he'd first feared – that the people who were home didn't know of the house, nor did they have an idea or knowledge of the old lady or even if she had once lived there. Finally giving up, Jim walked down the road to the nearby church in desperation.

The Reverend Stamshaw shook the hand of Jim, offering him a seat. "Right, Mr Turner," said the reverend as he looked over his spectacles, "let me see." Jim thought there was at least a chance of him knowing something because the old chap looked about a hundred years old! The reverend continued, "Mrs Audrey Tippins. Yes, that was the old lady's name. She lived there at the end of Castle Lane in her rundown house for years after husband George passed away. She used to be at church every Sunday, very independent, and she walked to the small shops every day, getting a few bits and pieces. Then, one week, she didn't turn up for church, and a few people commented that they hadn't seen her around the village. Eventually, I went with a small group of worried neighbours and a local constable to her house, and we managed to get in through the back door. The lock wasn't very strong, you see, and the constable made short work of it.

"Anyway, we slowly walked in, and her poor cat, I remember, was in a dreadful state. It had clawed at the door, trying to get out, and was nearly starved! But Mrs Audrey Tippins was nowhere to be seen. Not a sign of her! Even her hat and coat were still hanging up in the cupboard under the stairs, and at the door, there was a pile of unopened mail. I seem to remember the constable writing down that she must have left through the back door, because the security chain was still in place at the front door.

"But, also, it was confusing, because the key was still in the back door, which was locked from the inside. The key being in place meant that even someone with another key would not have been able to gain entry, and it still being in the door meant that she could not have exited and locked the door behind her. Anyway, after a few years, she never did turn up, and eventually, the house was in such a state of disrepair that her son, Frederick Tippens, decided to sell it to a local builder to develop the site."

Jim asked if he had an address for the surviving son, but the reverend replied, "I'm sorry, Mr Turner. I believe he was taken very ill with cancer a few years later. He never really enjoyed his wealth from the estate and died a few months after his diagnosis."

Far from tidying up any leads, Jim's investigation had just confirmed that there was, in fact, yet another possible missing person from years ago, a fourth. *What the hell am I looking at here?* he wondered.

Jessica arrived at work that morning with a glow in her cheeks and a purposeful stride. As she breezed in, Sarah Wilton noticed and asked her boss if she would like a coffee. Josh was back at work now after taking a few days to recover from the shock of losing his work colleague Kim, and he'd come back a driven man. Whereas before he would slouch into work, the young guy, slow to embrace the day, now he came in with extra purpose. His emotions had been ripped from him that day and been replaced by fear, guilt, shock, and a desire to find out the truth.

The white linen sheets which had been draped over the free-standing mirror were now whisked away by Josh, and Jessica was also right there, taking a close interest. Then Josh set to work on the frame, scraping away samples, cataloguing them, and then commencing their testing elsewhere in the lab.

Sarah, as Kim had done previously, checked the glass surface of the mirror, trying to pick up any trace of anything.

Jessica oversaw everything as they all endeavoured to find something, and as each test was done, Jessica's notepad quickly filled with comments, the page numbers increasing slowly, 47 – 48 – 49. Each detail was carefully noted until she reached around seventy pages. Then, as Sarah dusted the mirror and took sticky tape samples, Jessica noticed that Sarah had stopped moving, frozen as if time were standing still. Then she just flopped to her right, collapsing in a heap on the floor.

Jessica and Josh rushed to her aid, fearing she had knocked her head as she had fallen, although she had only been kneeling at the time. Her head had a large bump, and Jessica snatched her mobile phone and called for an ambulance.

By the time it arrived, Sarah was conscious again, but she

was groggy and not aware of what had occurred. As a precautionary measure, Jessica insisted that Sarah be taken to the hospital and checked over. The white linen sheet was placed back over the mirror again. Jessica's mind was in turmoil as she asked the paramedics to make sure Sarah had toxicology tests in case there were any poisons present, either as a gas or a residue that Sarah could have absorbed through the skin.

Jessica Linton was, in fact, quite upset, really. She was in charge and had to show some element of control, even if she was at her wit's end worrying how her young assistant had been taken ill; how could she have let it happen or not prevented it?

Once Sarah had been taken away, Jessica called Jim and said there would now be no more progress today. That done, she called Josh into her office and asked if he had noticed anything at all, and she also looked back at her notes, which had stopped at page 71.

The only thing she did find strange was at page 17, where her notes didn't seem to make sense. Instead of what she thought she had written, there was now just weird letters where it should have read:

"10-15 Josh scraping frame samples 7 bottom right corner light brown – 3.4 mm in length curled wood shaving covered in a varnish lacquer (to be confirmed) ETC."

It now read:

"10 – 5   /   s -C   P =-^_...;h l| woo d   r ou 3 mmm ."

Jessica read the next page, which was fine. Rubbing her eyes, she murmured, "How strange…"

Chapter 9

Julie Pendleton sat crying again on the end of her bed, her eyes sore from rubbing, her quiet sobs breaking the silence of the room like a knife. She was scared and upset. It was once again gradually getting darker, and from previous times, she knew that when it became completely dark, she would be asleep or unconscious for some time, which she feared, because she felt even more vulnerable than when she was awake. But however hard she tried to stay awake, she knew that it would happen, because it had happened before when the wall at the end of the bed had lit up and illuminated the room before eventually returning to darkness.

This cycle of events had now happened a few times. The first time Julie had gone through it was when the Chinese-looking man had stood there on the other side of the illuminated wall. It was as if they'd been separated by a huge, thick, misty window. He'd been writing notes and had looked up from his work as Julie had moved in closer to their glass barrier. He'd seemed in somewhat of a daze, stepping forward towards her and her room. At first, she'd recoiled in fear, not knowing him or what he was about to do. Then Julie had started calling out to him, "Hello! Help me, please!"

There'd been no reply, she'd heard no sound from the Chinese man at all. He'd stepped forward as if he was going to enter her room, and she'd recoiled further, holding her hands to her face, her eyes wide as she'd waited to see what would happen.

Would he step into her room or hit the glass? She had noticed he was dressed funny, like a doctor or something. He wasn't old, and although she'd been scared, he hadn't looked too worried.

There'd been no sound as he'd disappeared, as if melting into the glass like a misty wall, and once again, the view of her room had misted over. Julie had been so confused that she'd thought there were two rooms: she in one and another through the glass wall that had now gone again. She thought she was still in her bedroom, but when she'd looked past the Chinese doctor, she'd been able to see what looked like her room also, as a mirror image, or was she, in fact, in the mirror image?

The bed she sat on seemed different to the one she knew. It looked the same, but it wasn't. The sheets and pillows were more solid, like they'd been moulded as a total shape that had been painted. It was a false bedroom. It was light enough to see in the room, so she went to the door and clutched at the door knob, but like the bedding, it too was false, more like a solid-looking 3-D image, not real, like a picture. The whole of her room was like some show home; a pretend room, she had thought. So did that mean the real one had been on the other side of the misty glass? The room, false or not, had gradually grown dark, and with it, Julie had fallen silent, her calls, tears, and screams unanswered.

Time had slipped away, as had the light, and when it had grown dark, Julie had also been sort of switched off, maybe asleep, maybe unconscious. What she didn't know was that time had frozen – in fact, a day. The next time she'd awoken from her state, it had felt like only minutes had gone by.

As if waking from a dream, the wall had lit up with a low light, just a dull glow which helped her young eyes adapt. There were people moving around on the other side of the glass.

She could make out the large shape of a young, hairy-looking man on his knees at the bottom of the glass wall; then she also noticed two more people. As her eyes became fully focused, into view came a young woman, younger than her mum, and this woman looked straight at Julie, it seemed.

As Julie rubbed at her sore eyes, the young woman also rubbed, but at the glass wall that divided them. Looking past the two figures in front of her, Julie looked at the older lady, who was, perhaps, more her mum's age, more like her teacher at school. The older lady stood back from the other two, writing on a large notepad or book. All three were dressed in smart white coveralls, like doctors or something.

Julie watched on. She tried to call to them, but she gave up quickly, realising, as before, that people on the other side could not hear her. Then, the older lady's face changed, the look on her face glazing over, her eyes staring, just like the Chinese man's had. As she was scribbling her notes, she seemed to be in a daze, and she moved slightly forward. But then she shook her head and came out of the daze to carry on with her writing.

The wall misted, and the light faded once more. Julie called out yet again for help as it started getting darker and darker, but just as it went almost completely dark, it started to reverse the action, and the light returned, illuminating the wall of glass, making it brighter and brighter. This time, though, it was the same room and people in front of her.

The older lady looked wide awake, the large, hairy-looking guy was still on his knees like before, continuing with whatever he was doing, but the younger woman was now different: she was looking up towards Julie in a dazed-like state. Julie now knew the older lady had said something then, as the younger one had stopped what she was doing; she then seemed to faint, falling to her right – Julie's left – and the others rushed to help her.

Julie shouted out as loud as she could, "Help me too!"

But it was useless. It was like shouting at a television or something; they couldn't hear her, and she couldn't hear them either. She cried at her frustration and despair as, once again, the light started to fade.

For as long as she could, she pounded on the misting glass and shouted for help. The people on the other side were rushing around and panicking about their friend and colleague. Soon after, what looked like ambulance people and more doctor types in their white coats arrived. As the mist thickened and her false room darkened, Julie screamed and screamed, but the darkness didn't listen, ignoring her and engulfing the room in its cloak once again. Julie and the room fell silent.

Chapter 10

The ambulance pulled up at Southampton General Hospital with Sarah Wilton on board; she was sitting up now and talking to the medics, a large paramedic called Stan and a nurse called Liz. They'd checked Sarah's vital signs but hadn't found anything strange or wrong, but with the boss of the forensics lab insisting the situation needed to be taken very seriously, they'd thought it best that Sarah get taken to the hospital to be examined again with more extensive testing.

Arriving at the accident & emergency department, they asked if Sarah could walk without the aid of Liz, who offered an arm to assist with any stability required, but Sarah refused and managed to walk in completely unaided. Now, some forty minutes after the incident, she was feeling a little like a bit of a fraud. There was a total lack of symptoms from the mystery dizzy spell or whatever it was. Sarah knew deep down that Jessica was right to insist on her getting checked out. Who knew what the hell was going on with this, the strangest of cases.

Sarah felt very uncomfortable and self-conscious for jumping the queue, as she was called through to the medical assessment department and then, in turn, to a duty doctor for her examination. She felt even more uncomfortable with all the questions being fired at her and at being unable to provide much information to the medical staff, who were understandingly getting frustrated and confused as to what had happened and to what they were being asked to provide in testing and medical care.

Sarah suddenly heard a familiar voice, and to her relief, Jessica eventually appeared. She'd followed the ambulance to the hospital, and once there, it had taken her a little time to park. But she was here now, and she swung immediately into "boss mode", asking for a specific consultant that she knew of and specific tests to be carried out.

Although Sarah didn't normally like such a fuss, it was easier to let her boss do all the insisting of the medical tests. So, with a mixture of embarrassment, confusion, and relief that she was feeling loads better, she just sat back and let it all happen, resigning herself to the circus of attention.

Dennis Presswick had been a journalist all his working life. Now in his fifties, he had quite a network of informers throughout the UK and sometimes even further afield. The phone call he had just received was a sniff of a story, but that was quite often the way these things started. He was outside a café, grabbing a coffee along with an afternoon snack and heading back to the car, when Jezz, who worked at the local hospital as a porter, called with a "titbit". It was a little sketchy, but it seemed like a doctor from a forensic lab had collapsed after possibly being overcome by fumes, and there were doubts as to what had really happened, which had caused him to call. It had also been mentioned, in the conversations he had earwigged, that they wanted a serious number of tests carried out, and the fuss from the forensic manager also seemed strange, as if there was far more to this incident than was readily apparent.

So Jezz had kept an ear on them for some time and heard sentences that suggested it was part of the larger enquiry into the disappearance of an eleven-year-old girl, and also a lab assistant who worked in the same lab. *This is like finding footprints in the mud outside a murder victim's window*, he thought, and then, *I wonder what's in the lab*.

Stuffing the rest of the Cornish pasty in his mouth to free his right hand, Dennis opened the door of the black saloon car, not worrying about his greasy fingers on the handle, and slid in holding a coffee in the other hand. He was looking to put it in the middle between the two front seats, but the double cup holder was already full of empty cups, just like the ashtray which was also full, so full it might have accounted for the ash that had been deposited on the floor. Instead,

Dennis simply chucked an empty paper cup on the floor on the passenger side of the car, where it settled in the ash after rolling to a stop. He then sat the fresh cup of coffee in its vacated spot, next to an old cup which cultivated a layer of grey and green furry penicillin.

His black trousers were now being rained on by his mouth, which was discarding flaky pastry from the hot pasty. Other pieces tumbled down his grey round-necked jumper that covered a white shirt, of which a worn, grubby collar was all that was showing.

He fumbled around with his keys and turned them, starting the car, which coughed into life just as he also coughed, sending a few lumps of swede and potato to splat onto the dash.

After a quick look in the rear view mirror and a brush of his hair with his greasy hand – not the other, coffee-and-nicotine-stained hand –he squinted at the road ahead, signalled, and was away.

The poor old car chugged along, bellowing out smoke, a symbol of a man very much like his car: old, dirty, and clapped out, but which usually got where it was going with a dogged determination.

Hopefully, my determination will prove fruitful this time too, he thought as he arrived at the laboratory. It would seem to most people a difficult task to get past security at such a place, but Dennis had lots of years of experience.

With the light just starting to fade, Dennis pulled up at the security kiosk and confidently flashed one of his many ID cards. He explained he was there to collect an urgent sample for the hospital, throwing in a few random names along with a couple of names he did know, like Jessica Lindon's, which held some authority over the site. Then Dennis tipped the balance his way by offering £50 and clarifying that it was to save him a bollocking, because he should have been there sooner and now his job was on the line.

"I'll only be a matter of a few minutes," he said. "I might even get in there and find out someone else has already collected it." As he looked at the guard, Dennis knew he was wavering, so he added, "You can come in with me if you like? I won't be touching anything without your say-so. How's that?"

The young security guy asked his mate to watch things while he took a "ten-minute break".

"Right, fella, you've got ten minutes. Come with me." With

that, the guard let him park his car and escorted him to Jessica Lindon's section of the building.

Having bluffed his way in, Dennis ambled along, explaining that once they were in, he wasn't quite sure what and where a couple of the items were, but one was on her desk. They reached Jessica's section, and Dennis entered while the officer stood watching from the doorway. He wasn't that daft; he wanted to see exactly what was being removed under his watch. Otherwise, he could lose his job.

Jessica's desk was very tidy, which didn't help Dennis. *Really not much here*, he thought, and then he said to the security guy, "Ah, great. It looks like the report folder I was looking for has gone. That's good. Then all I need to know is that her other items are where they should be, and I can phone her and tell her everything is correct." He was thinking on his feet, the same feet that shuffled him about under his large frame and into the main laboratory.

Straight away, he could see a few things strewn about, abandoned when the lab assistant had taken ill. Some sealed bags on the table were labelled "mirror frame samples".

Standing on a white sheet, and covered with another white sheet, was a large object in the middle of the room, which obviously was the main focus of an earlier study.

Looking at the young security officer, Dennis gave out a guffaw. "Ah, this could be what Jessica was talking about." Walking confidently over to the sheeting, he said, "She told me just to check this."

The guard, at first, tried to stop Dennis from pulling off the sheet, but Dennis caught hold of it and whipped it off in one complete swish, like a conjurer, and it was too late. The object beneath stood revealed, a large, full-length free-standing mirror,

Dennis quickly proclaimed, "Yes, yes, this is it. I'm not going to touch it, my friend, but I was asked to check, um..." He looked desperate for inspiration, and he then saw his own reflection. Quickly, he said, "I need to make sure the mirror wasn't damaged in the earlier incident with the young lady," and with that, he didn't wait for an answer but simply set about looking around it. He spotted some notes that had been left on a single sheet of paper resting against one of its feet, under the main frame.

His eyes lit up. "Ah, there's the paper she mentioned. It wasn't on her desk after all." He tutted for effect. "Good job I saw that. I could have wasted hours!"

The guard was a bit uncertain, but when he looked at the sheet of notes, it didn't seem much of anything. Dennis read the sheet page as the guard looked around a little nervously. After all, if this weren't alright with everyone, it would be on his shoulders.

Dennis was unfazed and continued to pretend to know what he was doing, saying, "Oh yes," as he fumbled for his phone, distracting the guard by asking if he heard a noise near the door.

The young security officer looked away, which gave Dennis an opportunity to snap a photo of the page of notes, at the same time chuntering on about the paperwork and at times throwing in names at random. Once done, he slipped the phone discretely back into his pocket. The security guard was now over by the doorway, but he was keeping an ear on Dennis as he peered down the corridors outside the main room.

Dennis muttered away as he looked into the mirror, continuing the acting with, "That's the, um, five fifty-three with a—"

The room fell silent. The young guard gave a final glance up and down the corridor outside the main laboratory door and then turned to walk back into the room, just a mere two steps.

The note that Dennis had been holding was now on the floor, as it had been before their visit to the laboratory. The mirror was still uncovered, but there was no Dennis Presswick.

The guard panicked. "Where the fuck are you?"

His expletive went unanswered. The fairly large area was silent and empty. Dennis had gone. The young guard picked up his radio and called his colleague for help, not only for a quick search for the fat guy, but also for some moral support, but all he could think was, *What the hell am I going to do if he stays missing?*

Jessica lay back on the sofa, her shoes kicked off, a glass of red wine in her hand. The day hadn't been too good, what with her other assistant now in the hospital, and she had been late getting home for the takeaway she'd ordered. She sipped at her drink and physically and mentally sighed.

She looked down through the candlelight as her feet were being massaged by Jim, who asked, "How does that feel?"

He pummelled with his fingers and knuckles, and then stroked up and down her legs, getting ever closer to the top of her thighs. Then he started gently kissing, first her calf, then knees, then the lower inner thigh, and then the phone rang. It was Jessica's mobile that had sprung into life, not only its sound but also its light destroying the potential mood.

Jim tried to get her to ignore it, but Jessica had already picked it up. She looked at the screen, and recognising who it was from, she said, "I can't. It's from security at the laboratory. What do they want at this hour!"

Although it was now very late in the evening, Jim drove Jessica down to the laboratory, and they met with security.

The phone call she'd received earlier had been another mystery, as if they needed yet another puzzle. Apparently, they seemed to have one.

On the phone, the guard had said something about "a guy she had sent down there to collect a folder or something had simply disappeared." But it didn't make sense; she hadn't sent anyone to get anything.

Once she and Jim arrived at the lab, the guards explained that it looked like they had been duped into giving a man access to the lab. His car was still there, but there was no sign of him. Where had he gone?

Jim got on his phone and alerted his team. For a start, this guy could be hiding somewhere on the premises, although according to the security on site, they hadn't allowed access to anywhere other than the main lab and corridors to that part of the building.

They went through to the main lab, where the pair looked at the discarded sheet, which had been left to the side with the mirror exposed. Both Jessica and Jim examined the simple full-length mirror. What the hell?

At that point, the young guard's radio gate crashed their thoughts and concentration; his colleague was asking if it was ok to let in a three-car entourage claiming to be with Jim Turner's Unit. Jim said, "Yes, of course!" He was unable to hide his frustration, snapping, "Pity you weren't this cautious earlier when the other guy turned up unannounced." He couldn't help but have a bite at the incompetency that not only had denied him his pleasure but was going to lead to yet more work. At this rate, half the bloody country could disappear with idiots like them not doing as they should.

Jessica wasn't in a great mood either; it was her department that, again, had cocked up, and she couldn't help but feel embarrassed, possibly more because it was all in front of Jim, whom she felt she had let her guard down to. This made her question her focus. Was her attention elsewhere affecting her job, her judgement. They decided to leave the scene to Jim's team and take a look at the CCTV recordings in the morning,

Once outside, Jim held Jessica in a comforting embrace, being out of sight of his team. "Are you ok?" he asked.

She answered with a concerned look on her face, "Yeah, I suppose, so... look, Jim, if you don't mind, can you drop me off and leave me to myself and my thoughts tonight?"

After a small pause, he said. "Yeah, sure. Is it something I've said?"

Jessica replied, "No, it's just I'm worried about all this, and I don't want anyone coming back at us questioning our focus on such an important case. It's getting so mixed up."

Jim's face dropped big style, but he sighed and had to concede that she was completely correct. If they weren't professional about all this, then the press and their superiors would "tear them up for arse paper".

So, reluctantly, Jim shrugged his shoulders, kissed her on the cheek, and said, "Come on. Let's get you home." she smiled at him, relieved at his understanding, and he continued, "Perhaps the quicker we solve this, the quicker we can get back to us again?" Jessica nodded, but she didn't seem to be as certain of her thoughts to be able to return his reassurance.

Jim woke the next morning and punched the button on his alarm clock. He wiped his blurry eyes, blinking to get the focus, and looked at the phone screen, which showed him five missed calls already. Four were from his team, and one was from his boss, Chief Superintendent Neville Grieves.

Jim decided to jump in the shower and collect his thoughts first before returning their calls.

As he ran the water over the back of his head and neck, he sighed and thought that the one call he hadn't gotten was one from Jessica. As the hot water continued to massage his neck, he realised he was almost in a trance and that his mind was drifting. Realising it, he shook his head from side to side and quickly finished off.

A quick call to his team revealed that from the paperwork in the car left at the lab, the new and still missing guy who'd blagged his way in was a journalist called Dennis Presswick, which explained the motive of tricking his way past security at the lab. But they had also confirmed he was no longer on site. That fact wasn't good news, because it meant another had disappeared.

So now he had to give an update to the chief and tell him somehow that not only had there been little progress in finding the other missing people, but it looked like yet another had disappeared!

Good grief, he thought. *I wouldn't blame him for pulling me off the case or kicking my arse.*

Chapter 11

Chief Superintendent Neville Grieves was a hard but fair boss, but there was a limit to his patience, and it had been reached. Jim had come off the phone disappointed but not surprised.

"I've decided to add to your team a detective, Lesley Summers. She will be working with you starting tomorrow. I was holding off for a while, but after last night's new disappearance, it looks like I am vindicated in my decision to add to the team."

At least this Lesley Summers was the same grade as him and wasn't being put in over the top of him, although what she could bring to the team he wasn't sure. But he couldn't say too much when he had so little to go on.

Jim pulled into the station car park, and parked there in his spot was what he would jokingly call a hairdresser's car: a bright red Audi TT convertible. Parking to the side of it, he dragged his tired arse up the stairs and to his office, all the while keeping an eye out for the new fresh face that had been forced upon him.

There, half-sitting on a corner of a desk, attracting attention, from the male officers in particular, was a tall blonde smartly dressed in a white blouse and light grey suit. Lesley Summers appeared to be in her early thirties. She sat with a coffee in her hand, already looking very at home.

Breezing past to his desk, he purposely didn't look up until he had dumped off his bag and a couple of folders he had been carrying and then spun around and sat at his desk.

Lesley grabbed a chair and dragged it on its back two feet over the small distance to the other side of Jim's desk. But before sitting, she introduced herself, saying, "Hi, I'm Lesley. Hopefully you've been informed of my arrival this morning."

"Yes," said Jim bluntly, not wanting to concede any points in the introduction at all. His ego was feeling bruised enough already.

But Lesley just crashed on with the conversation and suggested they go for breakfast somewhere quiet and maybe catch up on where they were with everything. She had read some information the previous evening when she had finally gotten to her hotel room.

"Really," said Jim, "I'm not sure the parents and people that are missing can just wait around while we dine. But if you want a catch up, there is an interview room I'm sure we can use?"

Lesley didn't rise to the obvious jibe at her trying to break down the barriers and be friendly. "Okay, no problem. If you want to get straight down to it." Then she couldn't help herself, saying, "But remember, I have been brought in to help you! If the investigation wasn't perceived to be floundering in inactivity, then maybe you would have been left alone."

They headed for the interview room, her comment still stinging. Jim knew he was wrong, and her not standing for it had made him even more frustrated and irritable, but with the short walk, he had time to think. He also knew she was right; he did need help, but who likes to admit it. Walking into the room in silence, Jim turned as soon as the door to the room closed with a definite click and looked at her. Her face looked like she was in serious mode. *No friendly smile now*, he thought. *She's braced, ready for an argument.*

But Jim, recognising this, had a few moments to compose himself. His mind in overdrive, he came to the conclusion that he had better back down and quickly! He had turned to look down at the floor, and raising his head, he took a big gulp of air, sighed, and said, "Let's start again. I'm Jim. Fuck the room... Let's go get some breakfast. I will even pay for it, seeing as I've acted like a dick. How's that?"

Lesley thought about it for a split second and then said, "Okay, yes, breakfast is on you, and yes, you were a dick!" They then spent the better part of three hours chatting, with Jim outlining what had been happening and with Lesley suggesting a few points that could be looked at in more detail. She had to agree that from what she'd read from the reports, and now heard in Jim's brief, it did seem quite extraordinary, not only how the people had disappeared, but also the way they had carried on disappearing, like something out of a science fiction movie.

The phone rang in Jim's pocket. It was his team at the lab; there was CCTV footage of the moments before the disappearance of Dennis Presswick.

"We can take my car," said Jim. He was not about to arrive in a hairdresser's car in front of Jessica. He had some dignity left. It was bad enough his boss considered he needed help, but being driven to the lab wouldn't be good.

It didn't take long, and they were there, and they soon walked into the main laboratory together, an uneasy partnership, however brief.

Jessica was in her office waiting for them. When she spotted their arrival, she was curious as to who was now with Jim.

"Hi, Jessica," said Jim. "This is Lesley Summers, Detective Inspector Lesley Summers; she will now be assisting with the investigation." Turning to his side, he said, "Lesley, this is Jessica Lindon, who is in charge of this forensic laboratory facility."

Jessica extended a hand to greet Lesley, but her face didn't disguise her puzzlement. She quickly recovered her focus, but had to ask the question, "So, are you taking over the investigation, then, from Jim?"

"No." "No." Both Jim and Lesley were talking over each other in their haste to stop any confusion with the situation as quickly as possible.

"No, we will be just working together on this one," Jim finally managed to get out. Conscious of Jessica's quizzical persona, he wondered if there was jealousy or a rivalry angle developing from her perspective. He couldn't help but feel a twinge of devilment, and he emphasised his statement with, "Yes we will be working closely together now to see what we can come up with."

Jessica was quite flustered now, for once, but she showed

her visitors through to where Josh was sitting with a member of Jim's team. She explained as they strolled, "I think we're ready, indicating to Josh to start his laptop, which, on its screen, presently showed a view of the laboratory.

They were all glued to the footage played out in front of them on Josh's laptop. First, they fast forwarded it to when the security guard and the man they now knew as the journalist Dennis Presswick came into view. As it played, Jim looked up at Jessica, who glared at him in a playful rebuke at his earlier teasing, and he smiled back, glad she had picked up on it. It was his way of easing some of his bruised ego and also a way of introducing Lesley that didn't make him feel any more demeaned.

He returned his focus to the screen in front of them; they had finally gotten to the part where the fat journalist was reaching for the note. Picking it up, he looked over at the other side of the office. *Obviously, this must have been when he was distracting the guard*, thought Jim, in his mind matching the statement from the guard to the CCTV footage in front of him.

They all moved in closer, as if someone had given a secret signal to move, but in fact, no command had been given; it was merely that they were all gripped by the scene, waiting to see what had happened to him and hoping, finally, for there to be a breakthrough.

Their eyes widened, as there was a general feeling that the moment was close. They could see the journalist looking at the note. There was no audio to accompany the footage, but the movement of his lips could just be made out. He then appeared to stand transfixed, staring at the free-standing mirror right in front of him. He was frozen to the spot, not looking left or right. Then, without moving his lips or giving any indication he was about to move, he stepped forward, right up to the surface of the mirror. There seemed to be a bit of light emitted from the mirror, which was reflected in the journalist's face. Then, as they all stood transfixed like the Journalist in front of them, he moved forward again. The viewing angle they had of the scene was from above and to the side a little, and as the journalist moved forward, his large frame seemed to be almost devoured by the mirror.

The guy was large, and the mirror was narrow, possibly only an inch thick, and of course, the camera's view was along the thickness of the frame. But, like a magic act, they watched him disappear into the mirror until there was no sign of the guy left at all. After a short pause, the guard was then seen in the picture again, coming into view, looking around frantically.

Jim broke the stunned silence with the request, "Can you play it again, please? But slow it down at the point when he seems to disappear into the mirror."

Josh looked up at Jessica for confirmation to do what had been asked. She, of course, nodded her approval once she had jolted herself out of the stupor she had been in since watching the scene unfold. They all stood there, again and again, watching the footage. There was no doubt; he, the journalist Dennis Presswick, seemed to slide simply into the mirror and vanish!

Lesley asked to see this mirror that was causing such a mystery. Jim and Jessica also tagged along, although they had, of course, looked at the thing so many times now that they were getting fed up with it, having not gotten any closer to knowing what was so special about it. Eventually shaking her head, Lesley gave up staring at what looked like a very ordinary mirror, as had they all. After all, it looked like nothing special, just a fairly plain but old frame with minor swirls here and there, a darker wood, claw-type feet, full in length, and which could be tilted slightly from the middle pivot point.

Turning to Jim, she asked, "Who made it? Any idea?"

Jim said, "No, not really. It has no signature or markings, and we've only a general idea of age."

Lesley then asked, "Could it be, say, a magician's prop?"

"Well," said Jim, now feeling a bit on a back foot, as he hadn't thought of that line of enquiry, "I can ask someone to look at it from that profession, but I'm also wary of anyone else getting close to it at the moment, especially with Sarah Wilcox in the hospital too."

Lesley jumped on the last comment, the thought crossing her mind that Sarah could tell them something, since she'd been affected by the mirror but had not vanished like the others. Jim turned to Jessica and asked, "Didn't you say you had some sort of episode in front of the mirror too?"

Jessica said, "Yes. I had it while taking notes as Josh and Sarah worked on the mirror."

Jim asked, "What about your notes? This journalist also had a note in his hand before his disappearance. What about Sarah? What activity was she doing prior to her feeling unwell?" Running with the thought, he expanded it, asking, "Kim, wasn't he also taking notes? Was something you were all writing, or the actual pens, paper, and their close vicinity to the mirror or glass a factor? Was anything triggered? There was a definite glow emitted from the mirror as the journalist stepped towards it, but with no power supplied to the mirror, how is that possible?" Every time they seemed to discover a clue, no matter how tiny, it also started another list of questions.

"One thing I agree with all of you," Lesley said "is that we keep it covered up with a sheet and we restrict access to it to a minimum. We've got to control who goes near that bloody thing! More security, and we leave it here. I don't want to risk moving it or involving too many more people."

Jim, agreeing with everything Lesley had added, looked up at Jessica and wondered what her opinion would be. Even though he wasn't comfortable with Lesley throwing her weight about, she was right, so he couldn't say a word. This made him worry that he looked diminished in some way in front of his new lover, who had gone a little cold on him.

As he came away from the lab, Jim came to the conclusion that he had to up his game, get control, and solve this case. Lesley was right, but she was now possibly a threat, not only to his authority, but also because he could be seen by Jessica to be subservient, which wouldn't do.

The dark had lifted, and Kim woke, or rather came alive, as if a switch had been thrown. He was already standing, which seemed strange, and when his eyes focused, he found himself standing in a room. As the light improved, he could see it was the room of the little girl Julie Pendleton, where he thought he had just been working. His mind now raced to try to remember how he had gotten there.

What had just happened? He struggled to think clearly; he could remember taking notes and dusting the mirror, writing down some numbers, looking up at the mirror, and then his mind went blank. The light was coming from what appeared to be a glass wall in front of him, which was now sort of misty. The grey swirling mix in front of him emitted just enough light that he could now take full stock of himself and his surroundings.

He seemed unharmed, apart from feeling bewildered; he was still dressed as he had been when working in the young girl's room, in his white forensic coveralls.

He could now see properly in detail, and he looked at the door, which looked the same as before. At first glance, it had seemed white panelled with a chrome silver handle, but as he approached it, he could see that the handle now looked false; it was merely a representation, as if someone had photographed the door. It was actually identical, but it was just an image. Now up close to it, Kim studied the whole door. Every panel, instead of being raised with mouldings, in fact was now totally flat. His hands, carefully at first, touched the door; it felt solid, smooth. There were no edges to the door, no panels, and no protruding handle. It blended seamlessly into the rest of the wall. In fact, all the walls were the same, all like a photo image, he kept thinking.

He turned and faced again the one wall that was different, the wall not like a picture, the glass wall that was a swirling mass of... what?

It cleared a little in front of him, and he stepped closer. There was an image forming, and gradually, he recognised the scene. It was the laboratory, and in front of him, he could make out Sarah, Josh, and Jessica all peering in at him, but it was soon obvious that they weren't aware of him, and although he shouted and waved, they didn't notice his efforts at all. Jessica, for a moment, seemed to look straight at him in a glazed stare, but then she continued taking notes.

He gave up shouting for a minute and watched Josh, working away, and Sarah, who was even closer; then Sarah stood up and looked at him. She seemed to be in a trance-like state.

Kim jumped up and down, waving; she seemed but inches away from him, but she also seemed to look straight through and past him. As she stood there, she closed her eyes, her legs gave way, and she collapsed.

Kim shot a hand out to try and grab her to stop her falling, but his hand hit the wall. Although glass-like, it was so solid that it hurt his hand a little as it collided with the unyielding surface. Sarah, now on the floor in front of him, was being tended too by Josh and Jessica; he was concerned for her; even though he was seemingly trapped himself, his concern was genuine for his colleague and friend.

Soon, he realised his attempts to contact them and get help were in vain. The misty wall clouded back over, and the light started to diminish again. He quickly took another look around the room as the light faded, grasping at the smooth, glossy walls, the bed, wardrobes, and bedside tables. They were all false. He couldn't open any of the drawers or doors; they were all the same, like a picture or a show home, just a representation. His fingers couldn't pull them back, as there were no edges to grasp hold of.

As the small amount of light dwindled, he finally sat down on the solid bed, looking at the almost fully dark scene. The mist had thickened on the once glass wall until it was like a cloak of darkness that devoured everything. Kim didn't fall asleep; it was as if, when the light had gone, that he had been switched off, until, perhaps, the light returned.

The slight advantage was with Jim. He felt he held the upper hand in the investigation, possibly only for a while, because he had, of course, started it and knew a lot more information, particularly the people involved. He could not be seen to be slow and dragging his heels. Jim thought about the information he already had to hand that Lesley was keen to investigate and expand upon further.

One of the lines of the investigation were the notes Sarah and Jessica had written in their notebooks. Then there was also Kim's notes, all documented and available to Jim on his laptop. He gave a big sigh and then decided that the notes were where he would start. With that, he printed off the pages, and he then set them out with a label next to each with their names.

Sarah Wilton.

Jessica Lindon.

Kim Lee.

Each set of notes seemed to have a little substance that linked them together. *But*, he thought, *what about the fact that they all contained numbers?*

When Jessica had "felt strange", she appeared to have been on page 17, which, in her statement, she had mentioned. Sarah Wilton, when she became unwell and fainted or whatever, Jessica had mentioned the number 71. Kim, in the notes he had left on the floor, had noted 3 and 37. Then, thinking of numbers in general, Julie Pendleton also had numbers as a text that she had punched into the phone, the numbers 37. *Hmm, the number 7 was there each time*, he pondered. His mind then jumped to the journalist Dennis Presswick. He'd picked up Sarah's notes; he hadn't actually written any.

He flicked his laptop back on to the CCTV footage, which he rewound and played the few minutes before the journalist's disappearance. Then he played it several times through, peering closer and closer at the screen. The journalist was saying something as he read the sheet of notes. Jim then checked the young guard's statement; he had said that he'd known when the journalist "fell silent" that something had happened. *So what was he saying?* From his office phone,

Jim rang Trevor Symons, asking, "Can you please get me the contact details of the young guard at the laboratory."

Stephen Foster, the guard, already felt guilty and afraid for his job, but now, being summoned to go to the police station as soon as possible "to go through his statement" made him feel very vulnerable. He asked Inspector Trevor Symmons if he needed any legal representation and was told that it wasn't necessary but he was free to call someone in if he needed to. But Stephen couldn't help worrying that if this journalist was still missing, they were going to be coming after him.

Stephen sat down opposite Jim, who showed him just a small section of the CCTV footage, up to when the journalist Dennis Presswick disappeared. Jim stopped it before the clip got to him passing into the mirror; no way did he want all and sundry knowing they hadn't a clue what was going on.

After viewing the clip where Dennis was looking at the note and talking, Stephen was then asked, when he was looking down the corridor outside the room, what had he heard from the room and Dennis? Stephen thought a while and then said, "Sorry, I didn't take much notice of what he was saying. Just generally, he was in the background."

Jim persisted, saying, "You left a stranger alone in a room and weren't taking much notice? Really? Alone in a room with evidence, and you were the guard on duty and responsible when he disappeared? Look again," Jim said as he zoomed in on the picture to show Dennis's mouth clearly moving. "Think hard, young man." Stephen studied the footage, trying as hard as he could to recollect anything he could.

Jim prompted, "What did he say? He picked up the note and..."

Stephen replied, "I think he proclaimed, yes, this is what he was looking for to collect for Ms Jessica Lindon." The lead into setting the scene had worked a little; he remembered then that the journalist had repeated himself, saying again, "Yes, yes, this is it."

Jim prompted once again, "Did he call out any names or numbers?"

Stephen said straight away, "No, he..." Then he thought some more. "No, no names, but..."

"But what?" Jim coaxed. "Were there numbers?"

Stephen's face took on a quizzical look at the question. "Yes,

I think I did hear some numbers."

Jim pressed further, asking, "What numbers did he mention and in what way?"

Stephen replied, "No, not really. He didn't shout them out. I think now he was just babbling out random stuff not to cause suspicion. I'm really sorry. I can't remember making out any of the numbers, just a general sound that I can say sounded like numbers, not talk or sentences."

Lesley came to the door, tapping lightly. Jim thanked the young guard for his help and told him he could now go but that he might need to speak to him again.

As Lesley entered the room, she asked, "What was all that about?"

Jim simply said, "I wanted to hear if he had any more information now that we have the CCTV footage. I pressed him on the detail of anything he had heard the journalist say as he'd looked at the note or if he had called out to him. But there wasn't much at all." Jim wasn't being unhelpful. He wouldn't be that unprofessional when there could be lives at stake, although officially, the investigation was still classed as a missing persons and could well end up as anything, which could open the whole investigation up for scrutiny.

For now, though, he wanted to be cautious as to what "full" details he shared and when.

Once alone again, Jim contacted a professional lip reader by phone, apparently one the police department had used before in other investigations, as well as to secure convictions by giving evidence in court, a lady called Mrs Beverly Durant. She sounded like a bit of a fruitcake on the phone, but as long as he got the information he required from her, it didn't matter one jot.

This was all taking time that they didn't really have, but his thought was that one word or name could swing the investigation into the fast lane, or at least on the right road perhaps, and unlock this crazy mystery.

Once he had chatted with Beverly, he arranged with her to send an edited clip showing Dennis on the CCTV. Unfortunately, he had only been filmed from one angle, but there was a chance, which Beverly confidently predicted, that she should be able to capture some of the dialogue. Jim knew it could be a little tricky, as the guard had indicated that some of Dennis's words were mumbled, but Beverly just promised to do her best as quickly as possible. Jim was grateful and left it with her, just giving her his contact details, not the department's.

Looking at the ever-growing list of possible missing people, Jim's attention paused at the husband of the cheated-on wife, who had sold the mirror to the Pendletons: John Fisher. Jim let his mind flick and wander as he pondered if there was any connection between the different parties, however tenuous. With the Fishers, there weren't any notes or numbers showing prominence like with the others who had disappeared. He opened their folder on his desk, and as he did so, pieces of paper and notes spilled out onto his desktop. There were various sheets with details on the cheating husband and his new woman, who had been the victim's friend and whom he had now married, as well as the mirror sale from the auction. Jim's attention was drawn to the numbers on the mirror's receipt: its price, commission, lot number 351. Alison Fisher.

The other missing person he had even less of an answer too, of course, was the old lady who'd gone missing years ago – so many years ago that she possibly would be the hardest to find out what had happened too. She also had even less to do with all the latest disappearances, except, of course, the one thing that tied them all to each other, the mirror itself.

His mind wandered on its way, drifting, thinking now of the mirror, and he wondered what Lesley thought now after inspecting the mirror.

"The Great Alfonso", or Peter Wilson, which was the name he was born with, met with Lesley outside the forensic laboratory. As a senior member of the magic circle, he had been contacted by the detective inspector to see if he could "help with their enquiries". Peter, or Alfonso, had panicked a bit, his first thought being, had he or one of his fellow magicians done something wrong? Some parents and maybe others occasionally complained of being offended or worse, and with the big news stories of the day being focused on child sex abuse, it was a constant worry that even an unfounded accusation would or could destroy a career instantly.

The detective inspector was fairly quick to explain that they had an object that they wanted an opinion on. They needed to know whether it could be or had been used as a magician's prop, so they would like it inspected.

Peter was a slightly balding chap at fifty-two, and he had been entertaining people for many years. He had used props and, of course, seen lots of different types in all shapes and sizes. In particular, the inspector wanted to know if he had knowledge of the type used in making people disappear and general illusion. Peter, now confident there wasn't a personal problem, continued with explaining how he had had lots of props that made people disappear as well as sawed in half, and there were colleges he could refer her too if it were a specific make or genre, but he boasted that he was considered somewhat of an expert.

On his arrival, he was greeted by a very smart looking lady, tall, probably around six foot. He shook her outstretched hand as she introduced herself as Detective Inspector Lesley Summers. She was very attractive, he thought, in a hard, professional way, but at only five foot sex, he felt a little out of her league. Perhaps he also, still, was a little unsure of what was required of him.

They both walked from the security area to the inner laboratory and an office, where he met another smart-looking female who was in charge of the laboratory. Her name was Jessica, and she was not as tall as the lady detective, but she was just as attractive, he thought. Together, they all went down to the object, which was covered in a white sheet. Set aside, it stood on its own. Another white sheet covered the floor around it and under its small wooden feet that he could see partially protruding from the bottom of the covering sheet.

Lesley tried not to give away too much, describing the

situation as though they just wanted him to look at a large, full-length mirror that stood underneath the sheet and give an opinion as to if it was a magician's prop, but he was to take care, as it had "injured someone".

He was a little puzzled, but then Jessica pulled away the top sheet, exposing the now-infamous mirror to their scrutiny.

Jessica had her latex medical gloves on, and she handed a pair to The Great Alfonso. He paused but put them on anyway. It was strange, he thought at first, but if it made them all more relaxed, he didn't mind, and he wondered if it had to do with fingerprints or something.

There was very little conversation, he noted, between the two women, and he became aware the even with the people around in the laboratory, there was a definite sense of tension in the air. He looked at the mirror, feeling around the edges of the frame, pressing and probing with his covered fingers as he went, and then trying to slide it first to the left, then the right, then up and down. There were no switches he could feel. He took his time, taking his glasses from the top pocket of the old suit, putting them on, and peering ever closer at the frame. Jessica and Lesley looked on anxiously at first, and then they gradually relaxed a little as the small, funny-looking character pawed his way over every single inch of the frame.

His only indication to the waiting audience for an opinion was a grimace on his face, and occasionally, when he stepped back, he would take a moment to rub his chin as if he had an invisible goatee beard. Then there would be a little shake of his head, and he would continue.

Quite some time passed, and he had now been all around the frame, when, all of a sudden, the door of the laboratory opened and in came Jim. He strode quickly over to the gathering, asking once he stood next to them, "How is it going?"

Lesley introduced Jim to "The Great Alfonso". The magician looked up and shook his hand quickly. "Just call me Peter. Hopefully, I'm not performing at all at the moment," he said with a nervous chuckle that had the others looking at each other and wondering what the joke was meant to be, as none of them were the wiser.

"The funny guy" returned to his task, aware of the small audience he now had. He shuffled and stepped around and around the wooden-framed mirror. Then he ran his gloved hands over the back of the mirror. Its back was covered in a thin boarding, which he pressed, tapped, and tried to move from side to side. He then asked if it was possible to lay it down so he could inspect underneath the frame and legs. Jessica called Josh over to give them a hand, and once Jim and Josh had both donned gloves, they slowly let the mirror down so that the glass was facing downwards and resting on top of the sheet-covered flooring.

Once set on the floor, The Great Alfonso continued with a detailed inspection. He again ran his hands down the wooden frame and the back of the mirror's boarding. Then, to the newly exposed underside of the mirror, he pressed and rubbed, sliding and pushing. Then, finally, he inspected the feet, which were also made of wood. They had a claw-like foot design, all carved from the same piece of wood, as if part of the frame; they weren't screwed onto the frame but seemed to be glued to it in some way. Again, with these too, he tried twisting, pushing, and pressing them all ways to see if they moved to unlock a mechanism of some kind. But, after trying for a while, he had to concede there was no sliding or a click of a hidden engineered lever or movement to release a compartment. Finally, he requested the mirror be turned over to expose the front glass.

Once the mirror faced upwards, he knelt over the glass, going over every inch of it, pressing and tapping on it. Finally, after what seemed like ages, The Great Alfonso stood up straight for a moment as Josh asked if he could get anyone a coffee. Jessica spoke, offering the first choice of Josh's refreshment to her magical guest, who jumped at the chance, shouting out, "Oh, yes, that would be splendid!"

He was relieved a little that the tension of everyone standing there watching him had been broken by this small, kind action from the young man. He was also relieved because, under that intense scrutiny, his mouth had gone very dry. Relaxing a little now, he started to spring back into life, and he recognised he was the focal point of the scene, albeit for five minutes, which started to bring out the showman in him. He explained that he couldn't reveal trade secrets, but some backs of boxed frames had holes in them so as to make objects appear to slide through a solid surface, like the mirror, but he hadn't, as yet, found a thing. He was almost certain the mirror was, in fact, just a plain old mirror.

Jessica, Lesley, and Jim all seem to breathe a collective sigh. Jim shrugged his shoulders as Josh appeared with their coffee. The Great Alfonzo took his and set it down on the floor, thinking it too hot for him just yet after taking a small sip. He then knelt back down and continued to look over the upturned glass side of the mirror. The group sipped at their coffees, and they relaxed a little as the magician continued to study the mirror. Jim looked at Jessica and gave her a smile, which she reciprocated after only the briefest of moments. He had hoped the momentary pause in their fledgeling romance had not been extinguished before it had really begun. *Will it finish up as an on-off type of friendly liaison now and then?* he wondered.

He did notice that Lesley had quickly gotten very chatty with Jessica. He was almost disappointed that his little effort to tease her with a new, pretty female on the scene with a similar professional-woman persona hadn't gotten her just a little bit jealous, or even feeling she should renew their liaison sooner rather than later.

The Great Alfonzo took another sip of his coffee, this time a longer one, as it had cooled slightly, and he then bent forward, his glasses pushed back to keep them from sliding off his nose as he knelt over the mirror, his hot breath condensing on the glass. He then exclaimed to the group, "Wait a minute!" They all stopped their chatting, turning their attention to the character on the floor who was peering ever closer into the mirror, and waited.

The magician knelt upright. "I don't think this mirror is a movie prop at all. But..." He paused, took a big gulp of his coffee, and breathed onto the mirror's face, telling the group that he could make out something as his breath condensed on the glass. They all peered at the glass together, trying to make out what he was talking about. A small set of numbers appeared in the magician's condensed breath, and they kept appearing each time the magician blew his hot breath across the mirror.

Jim stepped forward. "Hang on a minute please." He took a sip of his coffee and tried to do the same, but no numbers appeared for him. He asked the magician to try again. The Great Alfonzo took a huge gulp of his coffee and blew, but unlike Jim, the numbers appeared once again. "There you go. See? Just like magic! Abracadabra 0571!" He called, and while watched by the enthralled group, he fell forward as if hit by sniper's bullet and was quickly swallowed into the mirror, with the glass swirling and glowing momentarily as his feet disappeared.

The onlooking group rushed forward, but they had no chance of grabbing The Great Alfonzo as he plunged into the mirror before their very eyes, just as if he had plunged into a pool. They were gobsmacked! They all stood about in silence, open mouthed, until Josh blurted out, "Fuck me! We've lost another one!"

The mirror clouded back over and then cleared into its original state. "A plain old mirror," Jim mumbled, now on his knees. He tapped the glass but felt he couldn't shout out "Alfonzo, where are you?" So he didn't. He felt that although the glass felt slightly warm to the touch, it was pretty much the same now as it had been when he'd first seen it. "Pete! Peter Wilson! Can you hear me?" Nothing. There was no reply. Just like all the others, he had gone!

Chapter 12

Jim and Lesley headed the rest of the team, along with Trevor Symmons and Simon Horn, into the office of Chief Superintendent Neville Grieves. After hearing about the latest incident, he'd seemed to take it very personally, to say the least. He'd simply cut the conversation on the phone short with the directive, "I want the whole team in my office tomorrow morning at 9 am." The only hint from him on his perspective were the words, "What a mess."

They all expected it to be bad, but as had happened many times before, when the circumstances were that bad, instead of a huge shouting session, in fact, it had gone beyond that to a level where it was quiet, which made it more menacing. They filed into the office, and noting the lack of chairs, they all decided to stand, realising that if they were the only ones to sit when they were probably looking at a difficult situation, then the wrath could easily be redirected at them.

This was as bad as it could get, really, and when Neville Grieves entered the room, you could scrape the tension off the walls with a knife. Striding purposefully to his desk, he didn't say a word. He took a fleeting glance around the room and slammed a file down on the desktop, making everyone blink. Then he said, "Right, Lesley. You were brought in to help make sure this investigation improved, to give a new perspective perhaps, but, above all, to back Jim up and to make sure that NO ONE ELSE, I repeat, NO ONE FUCKING ELSE, CAME TO HARM! Have you done that?"

"No, sir," was Lesley's offering. There was no point at this juncture in trying to defend the indefensible position that she had found herself in.

He then rounded on Jim. "Right. As for you, Jim, bloody hell! Was it your idea or Lesley's to bring in the 'Great Alfonso' for Christ's sake!" Before Jim could answer, Neville Grieves carried on with his tirade.

After it was over, they all sloped off, heads a little down, but they wisely saved their comments for outside. Once they did get outside, Jim and Lesley grabbed hold of Simon and Trevor and convened their meeting, frantically trying to come up with something. Jim said he would chat to Jessica again and make sure that mirror access was limited to only themselves, and even then, they would only go near the thing as a group. Lesley asked Trevor and Simon for any background on 'Al Fonzo', or Peter Wilson, or anything more on the mirror. He suggested they circulate a photograph of it to various antique dealers, and maybe go back to the church area where the first suspected case was recorded, the old lady who had disappeared. No more so-called experts were to be allowed access to the mirror without the super being in on it. He couldn't criticise then.

Lesley didn't have much to offer after her personal dressing down; she felt a bit lost. She had hardly come to grips with these peculiar events when she'd been judged for not getting anywhere with them. Jim had seized the moment, once again gaining the control of the investigation, but where did that leave her? Jim said he would go to the super with what was a bit of a plan and asked if Lesley had anything else to add. Lesley knew this wasn't good; it would look a bit lame and without direction, but that's how she felt, so she just murmured, 'No, that's fine.' Lesley then thanked Jim for taking it on, because she knew if she went into the super's office right now, there was a chance she would be in tears and look clueless.

Jim knocked on the super's door and entered after hearing an indistinguishable sound. Sitting down, he was invited to produce the "master plan" as to what the fucking hell they would look to do now on a one-to-one situation. When the atmosphere was a lot calmer and collected, Jim outlined his "bit of a plan", as it was.

Neville talked to him more easily now in private, though, of course, he didn't backtrack from his previous position; he simply eased it into a "team" effort to get them all out of the shit! After all, the press, as well as the victims' relatives, would demand answers, but the investigating team were only human, just doing their best. They hadn't produced answers soon enough, so the knives would certainly be out. For this reason, Neville Grieves had to share the blame with his team. Deep down, he knew they were trying to sort the mess out, but he piled on the pressure to Jim, saying, "You know we're under pressure to produce results. I'm going to come down personally to look at this mirror thing, just because I need to show I'm taking an interest, but I'm also fronting the press. What the fuck do I say? It's getting embarrassing, Jim. Put it this way, if this blows up in my face, it's your job on the line too."

Jim fully understood, and although, like in any industry, shit rolls downhill, he knew that if he were in the same position as the super, he would be demanding results. Everyone was frustrated by the lack of progress, but at the end of the day, he had to think of the missing people and their relatives.

Eventually, there would be a resolution to the weird events, but until, then he and others had to show they were doing all they could and were trying their best at all times.

The end of the day couldn't come quickly enough; Jim left the office dejected and down, but not defeated. It was now early evening, and his thoughts were clouded by his need for food. Then they turned to whether Jessica would be up for a meal together and if it would only serve to rekindle thoughts of work, because he desperately needed to escape from work for a minute. Jim reached for his phone and texted Jessica: "Fancy a meal together? Only one condition, the subject of work is banned! lol for that concession I am willing to pay xx."

He drove home and was getting sorted when he noticed his phone on the side light up with the reply. He read: "Ok Jim but just a meal. I feel so bad about the events I'm stressing so much at the minute, my boss is talking about our licence being revoked for incompetence, and Kim's parents have been in touch asking where he is and wanting to know what is being done to find him."

Jim read the long message and then texted back straight away: "Sympathy big time. My superintendent is giving me shit, please can we meet I need a cuddle?"

Jessica texted back: "Yes, of course, Jim that sounds gorgeous exactly how I need to feel right now, a cuddle and to feel loved :-)xx."

Jim read the last text, and although he was the one who'd mentioned a cuddle, he stared away at the word leaping off the phone at him: "loved". He halted himself before answering. He didn't want any missed understanding here, or to offer a false impression that a deeper relationship was on the horizon, but he had to concede to himself that he did crave company and the emotional comfort it could bring him. He simply replied: "Ok see you in a while meet you there 8ish xx."

Meeting for their meal, it seemed like they were back to square one. They had been close before, but now it seemed they were more like friends who just needed each other. As they ate and had a couple of drinks, they chatted about almost anything to avoid talk about work but also about their previous intimate liaison. Trouble was, the circumstances had changed the pressure of the situation too, which meant there was more than sexual tension between them.

The chilled meal helped a little. They finished, and as they walked to the cars, their minds were on how to address "the elephant in the room" or even two – one being the relationship and the other the work. *Can we make a proper relationship work*, Jim thought, *at the same time as we carry out our work?*

He knew Jessica had put the brakes on – and rightly so while all this was going on – but after this case, this would probably happen again at some time in the future.

They arrived at their cars. This was the moment when they would generally talk, as they had walked in silence on their way to the cars. The two of them stopped, turned, and then looked into each other's eyes. They kissed without words, hugging as they did, and both felt a bit vulnerable at the moment. Nothing needed to be said, really; their embrace said it all. With its intensity, it could have lasted forever as they slid further into one another's arms. When they finally relaxed their hold, their legs nearly buckled.

Solutions had to be found to the work-related problems, but at that moment, it was just them, together against the world. It didn't seem right to try and take it further; it was far deeper than that. Sex can provide superficial reassurance at times, but the embrace had gone deeper to their hearts and bones. As they parted, they were quiet. They knew they had perhaps a more solid foundation to their fledgling relationship than either really had realised up to this point.

Walking to his car alone, and though he'd sort of hoped to re-ignite the hot sex again, Jim was also happy there was something between them. Only time would tell how deep it was and if, after all this latest mirror crap had passed by, they could re-ignite the fire which had previously sparked, but for now, a warm, secure glow between them would suffice. As they left in their separate cars, the night drew to a close. The meal and drinks would perhaps help them sleep, but it would still be more likely that the embrace they'd had while standing at the cars would help them stay asleep, as they were both a little more reassured for now. The following day wasn't going to ignite any fire – well, not in that way.

Jim and Lesley got to the forensic laboratory before the other detectives and took the opportunity to warn Jessica that the superintendent had decided to come along and visit what was now the main focus of the investigation: the infamous mirror. Jim and the two women, Jessica and Lesley, stood before it, all in a line. They pulled away the white cloth as they had done many times before and stared at the quite ordinary mirror. The thought crossed Jim's mind, *What if there is something obvious that we missed, and the superintendent walks straight in and simply just points it out?* As quick as the thought had come into his head, it was dismissed. *Good luck to him*, he decided. He was starting to get sick to the back teeth with the sodding thing!

As the three of them stood at the mirror, nothing much was said about it. Josh offered to fetch coffees for all, and Jessica temporarily covered the mirror up again while the others made their way to her office, where they at once engaged in polite chit chat.

They weren't there long before the outer door to lab opened and the chief superintendent walked through it flanked by detectives Trevor Symmons and Simon Hearn.

Jim and Lesley indicated to Jessica that this was indeed the super. Lesley quickly asked if the chief would like a coffee. His answer made her feel very uncomfortable, as he snapped – so that it was directed at all of them, really – "No, thank you; there's time for that later." Jim also felt a bit awkward, and being near a table, he immediately put his cup down on it, hoping it wouldn't be seen. Lesley felt even worse, now being the only one out of the team holding a cup, and she started moving it from one hand to the other like she was playing pass the parcel, as if it would explode if kept still for any length of time.

The super was focused on being forthright and in charge. He didn't linger, but straight away, as soon as Jim introduced Jessica Linden, he strode over, shook her outstretched hand, and introduced himself to her very formally as Chief

Superintendent Neville Grieves. He then apologised for the lack of progress so far and said that he was sorry that a member of her staff had also disappeared.

Jessica said, "Well, I think we are all in this thing together now, so the sooner we get it sorted, the better."

He agreed and enthusiastically confirmed this, replying, "Yes, yes, definitely. Right, where is this mirror, then?"

They all shuffled around and then strode over to the covered item in the middle of the main laboratory. its white sheet could not hide its shape, but it did, somehow, give the illusion that they had it in their ownership and under control.

Jim decided at this stage to just voice a concern, and he said, "Before we uncover it, can I just warn all that if there are any numbers like we have heard about and seen, it can be wise to back off again and maybe replace the cover?"

Lesley took the opportunity to discard her cup and then join them without being noticed. She chirped in after Jim's warning with, "Yes, I agree. Safety has got to be the priority."

Jessica and Josh together pulled off the sheet and handed it to Sarah Wilcox, who had just come over to watch the proceedings. Jim involuntarily held his breath, as if expecting something to happen, but it was such an anti-climax. The mirror just stood there as it had done before, so damned un-dangerous looking. It seemed so ridiculous and surreal, all of them peering in the mirror waiting for the super to say something.

After the pregnant pause, the super said, "Well, this is it then?"

Lesley and Jim said, "Yes, sir."

"And you say the magician, the latest to disappear, was standing just here?" The super pointed to a spot on the floor. After getting a nod of confirmation from Jim and Lesley, he continued, "In your report, it said he seemed to recite some numbers or something and then simply fell into the glass?"

"Yes, sir."

The super moved closer and tapped at the glass with the knuckles of his right hand, making a small noise. He announced to everyone, "It seems solid enough. Are you all sure that he didn't do some sort of trick, just for effect? What's this chap's background? Are we sure he isn't the real owner of the mirror and has duped you all, hoping to get publicity for his act?"

Trevor spoke up, saying, "We looked into his background a little yesterday, sir. He had a few bits on file, nothing was proven, though he'd had a few accusations of child abuse. Basically, he was accused of getting touchy feely with a few children in the past while performing his magic act. He was cautioned and monitored; that's all."

"Can we find any previous working partners and also a wife, lover, or whatever? Has he done an act or illusion with mirrors? If so, I want to know."

"Yes, sir," came the replies from around the room. There was no arguing when they could tell he was flexing his authority.

They all continued with minor observations until the super pointed out that the mirror had, in fact, misted a little. Squinting his eyes, he continued to observe, pointing with an outstretched finger and saying, "Are those some numbers there?"

They all diverted their attention swiftly back to the area being pointed at by the super. Jim, Jessica, and Lesley, almost as one, said, "Careful, sir, don't recite the numbers!"

He ignored the advice and read out, "It seems to be 17."

Although the mirror went a little mistier, nothing happened, and the super added to his dismissive attitude with an outstretched hand, knocking again on the surface of the mirror, making the point that it was still solid, and announcing, "See? Nothing is happening here. Must be the change in temperature causing it to mist."

Jim rolled his eyes at Lesley and shrugged his shoulders at the super's comments. Jim was feeling a little bit defensive of the mirror's worrying aspects and again expressed caution. But no, the Chief Superintendent was boldly stepping closer, exclaiming, "Are those more numbers?" and pointing again.

This time, however, it was Jessica who read them out: "5331." But, again, nothing happened, and she also tapped the glass front. The super did the same, agreeing with the numbers. But when he said, "5331," and tapped the glass – whoosh! First his arm, and then the rest of him, disappeared into the now swirling misty glass. Jessica was the nearest to him, and she tried to grab the super as he disappeared, but her hand, although the mirror was still swirling with mist, hit a solid surface. Jim and Lesley panicked, shouting, "Sir! Sir!" with Jim trying the numbers again, shouting, "5331!" and then, "17! Sir!" But there was nothing. The glass was solid. They all tried to reach in, as the mirror was still misty, but the glass was solid again.

Jessica piped up, "This is crazy! I touched that glass a second before him, also saying 5331, and it was as it is now." As she vented her frustration with trying to understand the situation, she repeatedly tapped at the glass and said, "17." With that, the mirror's mist thickened in an instant, and in the blink of an eye, she too was gone!

Jim couldn't believe his eyes. He couldn't understand. He too had been touching the glass and reciting the numbers, so why not him? He tapped, hammered, and finally pounded on the glass, calling for Jessica. He got more and more frantic, screaming at the object. Jim had lost it now that Jessica had gone. In desperation, he glanced around and finally grabbed a tall stool that was behind him and partially pushed under a workstation bench. Changing his hold from carrying it to wielding it like a club, he swung it at the intended victim, the mirror. The others jumped back, not wanting to get in his or the stool's way. His first effort bounced back at him. Increasing the ferocity, his second and third were more powerful again, hitting the surface in the middle and above center in quick succession. The second blow cracked the surface, and the third sent it crashing, with glass flying in all directions, skidding off the tile flooring. The hurried violence was then followed with silence, except for Jim's panting as he, like the others, stared in silence at what he saw in front of him.

Chapter 13

Jessica's head was still spinning as her vision cleared. Behind her was the swirling mirror, which she had been sucked through, and in front was what appeared to be her laboratory, where everyone had been standing moments before, but there was only herself now, standing alone, still feeling a little strange as she quickly tried to get her bearings.

She walked away from the mirror, its glass front now seeming to take up the whole of one wall. From her perspective, it looked now like a gateway which, unfortunately, had closed.

Jessica shuffled around the room, hesitant, as if puzzled not only by the lack of others but also by the fact that everything around her in the laboratory was false, such as light switches, drawers, equipment, etc. They all looked the same, but when you got close or tried to actually grasp them, they were, in fact, just like 3-D images, with no function, very lifelike until you went to touch them. *Like some kind of show house items*, she thought.

Then, as if suddenly woken from her thoughts, she remembered the superintendent. Where was he? She had followed straight after him into the swirling mist of the mirror, perhaps not by choice, but surely he should be there!

After going through the mirror, Chief Superintendent Neville Grieves was feeling confused and embarrassed to have succumbed to it. He looked around and tried to put his hand back through the swirling mist of the mirror surface, only to find, once again, that it was now solid.

Turning, he saw the laboratory he had just been in; the only difference, though, that he could see immediately was the fact that he was now on his own. He called out, "Jim! Lesley!" and then, "Anyone!" Something was different. He strode towards a desk, where he had spotted a phone, but after only a stride or two, he stood at a flat wall; the edge of the desk and the objects on it were just an image. *It's like being on a film set*, he thought, *with cardboard cutouts and wax fruit.* He wrestled with all sorts of things in his mind. Had he been the subject of a prank? Is this what had happened to the others? Was he awake, or unconscious, perhaps?

As he looked around, he shouted, "Hello!" After a while, he realised this was no prank, and he could well be in trouble. He started to feel very uncomfortable. Something was very wrong.

Alison Fisher awoke, if that was the correct word, from her stupor or suspended state, and like all the other times, it was to see someone at the mirror's glass-fronted wall seemingly falling towards her and the room, just as she presumed she had done when she came to be here, however long ago that was.

On this occasion, though, it was a little different, with two people in quick succession, one after the other. The first was a large, tall chap, possibly in his mid-fifties, in a uniform black trousers white shirt, and black lapels; he looked like he could be a police officer of some kind.

Then, as if trying to stop him, or maybe to follow him, a woman in her late thirties or early forties, in smart business-type attire, her mouth moving as if calling after the first chap, also fell towards her. Just like all the others Alison had seen at the glass-fronted mirror, the woman had a dazed expression on her face as she disappeared from Alison's sight. The glass then misted and swirled, and Alison knew that it would gradually darken until, once again, she was alone and had passed into a new stupor or suspension. Alison hadn't a clue how long she had been there. She felt the same each time the events played out, not tired not hungry, just existing. Sometimes, she thought she had only been there for moments, minutes, hours, but during some of the latest incidents, she had spotted newer-looking technology, and clothes and hairstyles seemed a bit different, which made her doubt what was happening.

The police officer had gone from view, and the lady, some sort of office manager perhaps, had as well. As the darkness fell on the room, something worried Alison. Every time this had happened before, she had felt enveloped in the descending darkness and had then slipped into an unconscious state, but this time, it was different. Something had changed. The mirror's glass wall had stayed a little lighter, light enough for her to make out her surroundings just about.

Also, she hadn't passed out. She remained awake and aware of everything. At first, Alison thought, *Is this going to be where I find out where I am, or is a door about to open?* She waited and waited. Things did feel different; she felt for the first time a presence in the dark room with her. It seemed to move around her silently, like a dark shadow, forming a shape for a moment and then, when moving again, it was formless, more like smoke drifting with no purpose or direction.

Alison felt scared and in danger. The hairs in her nose bristled as a smell reached them, and as the thick stench passed by them and into her nasal passages, it made her feel worse. The smell was like rotting meat. Something evil and threatening was in the room with her. Her heart raced, adrenalin pumping, and her body tensed. Then came the worst thing so far: a voice like a guttural, growling whisper. There was a hot, stinking breath on her neck. It made her shiver down her spine. She was terrified as she heard, "351, it's time for judgement."

Alison had tears rolling down her cheeks, and she trembled all over. She was so scared. She didn't scream, but with the hot breath so close, it made her lose control of herself. No longer alone in the dark, she was now standing in front of a very evil presence, so vulnerable, so afraid, and she let go of her bladder slightly. She was frozen to the spot, waiting for what would come next.

The broken glass was still sliding across the floor as the remaining detectives and laboratory assistants looked on at what was left. The wooden frame was still upright, and within its centre there was just a black void. Its appearance was more like tar, soft, rippling, but with the mirror still in an upright position, it seemed to defy gravity by not spilling out. It was like a black liquid pool held in suspension. Then, as they looked on, it twisted into shapes, and features defined themselves into a horrid face, not of this world.

Everyone in the room was silent, rooted to the spot. Then Trevor spoke. "What on earth is it?" he asked, but there was no answer forthcoming. They all waited to see what would happen next.

There was a smell filling the air that was horrible; it seemed to emanate from the black substance, which continued to mould and form into a face-like shape. It filled the inner frame of the mirror, its features protruding into the room a little.

They looked on quizzically until they heard it speak; then they recoiled away a step or so with the first words, which sounded vicious and evil as they were spat into the tension-filled room.

"I AM AIAKOS. THOSE CAPTURED BY THE MIRROR WILL NOW BE JUDGED. YOU CANNOT INTERFERE, FOR YOU ARE MERE HUMANS! CHOICES FROM THE PAST WERE MADE AND CARRIED OUT. I AM AIAKOS. MY JUDGEMENT IS FINAL."

Jim spoke up, directing his voice at the apparition, "What do you mean, 'judgement'? What have you done with them?"

His words were met with a stony silence. The tar-like face gave away no emotion and no indication of its intentions, and when the black liquid moved again to envelop the face back into the abyss, it steadied until it had become a flat, glass-like surface.

The surface continued to morph until it was a new, darker mirror, and then it started to show faint images as if it was now a large television screen. The images filtered through from deep within the mirror, becoming ever clearer and unfolding the full horror before the assembled mystified eyes. One by one, like thumbnail pictures that gently open and form clearly on a mobile phone, images started to appear in squares in the mirror. The square images formed into columns and rows while the extent of the pictures that were emerging grew, as did the group's distress at what they saw.

Jim and the others could now make out dozens of pigeonhole square boxes criss-crossing the mirror's surface, a bizarre collection of even stranger settings. As the group peered even closer, they could make out the people in each square. Each box-like square was like a glass-fronted room with a person trapped inside. The rooms appeared to be exact replicas of the same rooms the people inside had disappeared from. Jim recognised the bedroom of Julie Pendleton.

As they scrutinised the images further, they could see from some of the people's clothing, furniture, and technology that it looked like they had been trapped in time and space, some maybe for years.

The figures stood around four to five inches high. Jim and the others tapped the glass fronts and tried to talk to the small figures, but to no avail; the little people were oblivious to their attempts. The group was desperate to help or even understand what they saw, but from lack of reaction from the people on the other side, they could not hear the group's efforts to contact them.

Closer inspection revealed even more horror. One guy had hung himself, and another poor soul was just a skeleton; another, they could see, had smashed up his room, and the occupier was now sitting in the corner, as if he had been driven crazy from his incarceration.

Looking box by box, the group gradually made out each and every missing person they had spent the last few weeks trying to find.

As they pointed out people to each other, they could see the individuals were clearly now no longer in a stupor, not that Jim and the others were aware of what their state had been previously.

The figures seemed mostly to be pacing around their rooms, oblivious to the onlookers.

Trevor pointed to the chief superintendent, who was pacing about in his box, which looked identical to the laboratory they were presently in.

Jim spotted Jessica, who was also in a box identical to the lab, and he touched the surface, but try as he might, he couldn't attract her attention. He could see she was upset, distressed, and frustrated at her forced detention. Julie Pendleton sat in a corner, weeping, obviously afraid, as was Alison Fisher, her tears trickling down her red cheeks, but unlike little Julie, she stood, looking confused.

Others had started to pound on the glass surface, though no sound was transmitted through to the "real" laboratory. Their mouths open, screaming.

Studying the crazy scene before them, the group began to notice, in the right-hand corner of the glass-fronted wall of each room box, a number. In Jessica's case, it was the number 17, and in the superintendent's, the number was 5331. Alison Fisher had 351. Jim pointed to the bottom row, at young Julie Pendleton's 35. Josh then spoke up, pointing at his friend and colleague Kim, "Look. I can see a 337 here." They all continued looking, noticing that the magician and the journalist were also there.

Jim shouted out, asking the so-called "Keeper", "What are you going to do?"

No reply came. All they could do was wait to see what would unfold.

Once the recent activities had settled down, they wondered if the "keeper" might then put in another appearance. Would he make this "judgement"?

The group in the laboratory chatted as to what to do next and decided that for the people whom they could identify straight away, like Kim, Alison Fisher, etc, it could be a good move to inform their relatives that there had been a breakthrough and get them down to the lab. For some of the people who had been missing for years, there were medical implications, such as the shock of walking from maybe thirty years ago into the present day. Also, what if decisions had to be made with, say, Julie Pendleton? Legally, her parents would have to help make decisions.

The group could see from the trapped people's clothes that they were exactly as they'd been when they had first disappeared, suspended in their original state.

Those in the lab worked quickly as a team. First, there were cameras to set up to record what was happening, for they had no idea how long they would have to wait. The mirror had to be watched twenty-four hours a day.

There were so many individual squares in the mirror that it was like a mosaic of tiles, and they soon found it difficult to check on all the rooms at the same time. Lesley and Jim decided to write down the numbers and correspond them with each person's name. Then they got Trevor and Simon to follow up with contacting relatives. They needed to know everything about those stuck in this weird situation. According to Aiakos, they were about to be "judged"; did someone have a grudge or something, perhaps? Then there was the task of identifying the poor souls who were already dead.

Medical help was summoned quickly, but it caused its own difficulties. How do you explain the symptoms of people in a tiny box-like room being held under the strangest of conditions?

The detectives had their work cut out. In the end, Jim just

described it as a hostage-type situation that they needed to keep a lid on, but it could quickly change to needing several ambulances if it suddenly unfolded.

In the end, it was agreed to have two ambulances and their crews there ready to ferry casualties to the nearby hospital if required.

Josh broke the focus of the busy hustle and bustle of the group by yelling, "Something is happening!"

They all stopped what they were doing and hurried over to the mirror, which had suddenly clouded over in mist again to reveal eventually not the previous mosaic of squared rows of rooms but one room which filled the whole inner frame of the mirror. In the room, one man stood alone. This room looked like something out of the 1920s, with its dark furniture, a flower pattern lamp beside the bed, a wash basin, and a jug. On the back of a chair was what looked like an army uniform; it hung there off the chair in front of an open fire, at the right of the room as the group looked at it. The glow from the fire, with its logs alight, made it all look a bit like a scene from a film. The guy had a robe on, as if he had bathed or was about to go to bed. At a guess, he was perhaps in his early forties, with smart, short hair that was slicked back with maybe a dab of brill cream or something.

From his moustache, general demeanour, and calm disposition, Trevor made the observation: "Definitely an Englishman." As the man strode across the room to the other side, he had a slight limp. This was confirmed as he took hold of a walking stick which hung over the headboard of the bed. Then he stepped back to more or less the middle of the room.

He cleared his throat with a little, muted cough, and all in the lab looked on in silence, realising they could now suddenly hear someone from the mirror for the first time

Lesley was the first to try and attract his attention. Stepping a pace closer, she tried talking at the glass-like mirror. *It's like trying to communicate through a TV screen*, she thought. And just like with a TV, the verbal traffic only travelled one way.

The guy stood there, not moving much, shuffling his feet as Lesley said again, "Hello? Can you hear me?" No reply came back. She gave it one last go, saying, "Hello there! Can you hear me?" Still, nothing came from the chap in his room, apart from clearing his throat again. Probably, the cough was a small habit or, possibly, he smoked.

Lesley was now quite close to the glass. It seemed strange, him being on the other side of it. The mirror stood at around five feet tall, and the guy filled the area, unlike the figures from before, which had only been around four to five inches in height. Lesley tried one last time by shouting at the top of her voice, "HELLO THERE!" Nothing. He obviously could not hear them. It was established then that the sound was only travelling one way. They settled for just watching the goings on as a live TV audience at the filming set.

The silence was finally broken by the voice they had heard once before. "I AM AIAKOS," the voice boomed out of the mirror. The guy they were watching reacted to it by ducking instinctively at the sound, and the group quickly noted that both they and the chap had heard the voice simultaneously. They assumed that the voice was coming from inside the guy's room in some way. They then noticed that when he had ducked, he'd seemed to look up a little towards the left-hand corner of the room where it met the white ceiling.

The voice continued, "YOU ARE NUMBER 37335. IT IS TIME FOR YOUR JUDGEMENT. STATE YOUR NAME!"

The poor man was shaking as he stuttered, "Who, who, err, what judgement? I've done nothing wrong!"

The answer was unforgiving and relentless. It made everyone jump, as its volume had increased and it had become sharper. "STATE YOUR NAME!"

The man was trembling, but finally, he shuffled his feet and picked up his stick, which he had dropped when surprised by the first burst of Aiakos's voice. But instead of putting it to the floor to steady himself, he brandished it, ready to defend himself. Then he pushed out his chest and proudly proclaimed, "My name, sir, is Jonathan Steedle. Now, WHO ARE YOU?"

The voice came back at him again, this time less aggressively, but somehow, it seemed more menacing with its confidently controlled delivery. "I AM AIAKOS. THE MIRROR HAS BEEN BROKEN, AND SO HAS THE BOND. YOU MUST NOW BE JUDGED."

Jonathon repeated, "But I have done nothing, sir. Who are you to judge me? I'm in my own house. Now, show yourself!" There was no reply. Jonathan stood steadfast, ready to fight if he had to, his stick raised. But his resilience was simply met with silence.

Lesley quickly whispered to Josh, "Are you recording this?"

"Yes," came back the reply. "I've got it all."

Jim continued to whisper out orders to Simon, "Can you check out this guy Jonathan? Now that we have his full name, maybe we can get an idea of what he could be judged upon and, of course, what might happen if it was someone with a grudge. Also, can you see if he has any next of kin around?"

The group's hurried whispers were brought to an abrupt end as the voice of Aiakos started again, making all jump, startled by its booming volume again. "YOU, JONATHAN STEEDLE, UTTERED YOUR NUMBERS AND WERE CAPTURED BY THE MIRROR; THE MIRROR'S BOND WAS BROKEN. YOU HAVE NOW BEEEN JUDGED. YOU ARE NOW FREE TO GO AT ONCE!"

All in the lab looked at each other. This chap Jonathan looked about him, a bit confused. He then turned towards the front and took a few tentative steps towards the glass. In turn, those in the lab took a step back to accommodate his entry, the movement occurring altogether as one.

The mirror's glass-like surface swirled as it had done before. Then, as they all looked on in open-mouthed silence, first a hand appeared through the mist, followed by Jonathan's head and torso, and there he stood at his full height with a stick in his hand. He was blinking from the bright fluorescent lights of the lab, which were magnified by the white surfaces and tiled flooring.

Both he and those in the group stood in open-mouthed

surprise. As they went forward to greet him, he raised his stick, and with a trembling voice that almost got stuck in his throat, he quickly said, "Stand back! I warn you!"

They all stopped, except Lesley. She ventured forward a little more, extending her open hand and smiling. "It's ok, sir. You're safe now," she said, trying her best to reassure him.

He was acting just like a frightened rabbit caught in the headlights – not laboratory lights – switching his eyes from stranger to stranger and then flicking his head from side to side, not sure if he was about to be attacked, but ready as much as he could be for whatever was going to happen next.

"Where am I? Which one of you is Aiakos?"

Jim said, "Well, none of us is Aiakos. We are all police and medical staff, sir. You are quite safe, but there is a lot to talk about. First things first, if you don't mind, can I get you to sit down in the office?" Jim pointed at Jessica's office with a finger, but he moved slowly so as not to get Jonathan swinging his stick.

"We will get you a nice cuppa. How does that sound?"

Reluctantly at first, Jonathan moved away from the mirror one fragile step at a time. Jim beckoned over to Sarah to help, and they were both just in time getting to him as his legs gave way and he almost stumbled into a nearby desk.

But, supporting him on both sides, they helped him to the office and sat him down. Jim looked up, aware that Sarah wasn't his staff to order about, but he said gently, "Sarah, would you mind? Can I leave him with you a minute?" Jim then rushed back to the doorway and asked the others, "What's going on now?"

Josh answered him, "It's ok. I think it's gone back to how it was before, with all the boxes in rows."

Jim shouted over to Trevor, "Is that ambulance crew on site yet?"

"Yes," Trevor replied. "They're outside with the laboratory security."

Jim gave the ok to let the paramedics in now. He knew it was going to be hard for this poor guy to comprehend, but he wanted to get Jonathan relaxed a little and then, perhaps, get some information from him. If Jonathan was too shocked, Jim could maybe see him clamming up.

Jim returned to the office to find Jonathan peering around, his glassy-looking eyes wide, looking totally bewildered. Jonathan turned to Jim and asked, "So, you're a police officer?"

"Yes, I am Detective Jim Turner. I am trying to find some people who have gone missing for some time."

Jonathan looked even more puzzled, if that was possible. He replied, though, saying, "Well, I've been there in my house, sir, since Tuesday, I think. What day is it today?"

Jim thought a second and just replied, "Wednesday." He thought it better not to enlighten Jonathan further at this stage. But he said, "I'm sorry, Jonathan, but before you go with some medical people, I need to ask you some questions to help me find some other people."

Jonathan looked worried as he quickly asked, "I'm not in any trouble, am I?"

Jim smiled and answered, "No, sir, not at all. Now, enjoy your tea a minute. Sarah has just popped it on the table there next to the laptop."

"A what top?" Jonathan's face was still puzzled looking.

Jim smiled again. "Sorry. Next to that electrical device there." He pointed at the grey HP laptop sitting closed on the coffee table. Jim continued, "Now, that voice you heard calling himself Aiakos, have you ever heard it before? And, if so, would you have an idea whose voice it could be?"

"No, sorry. Today is the first time I have ever heard it."

Jim was aware he only had a limited time to ask maybe a couple of questions before he had to get back to the mirror, but he also knew the guy in front of him was totally bewildered. He pressed on, asking, "So your full name is Jonathan Steedle? And your age is…?"

"Yes, sir, my name is Jonathan Horace Steedle, and I am forty-two years old," came the reply.

"Where were you born, and what year was that, please, Jonathan?"

"I was born in Brighton." Jonathan smiled. "And you're not too clever at math, are you, lad? I'm forty-two, so I was born, of course, in 1885."

Jim noted it all down. "So, if I'm right with my rubbish math, is it 1927 then?"

"Yes, of course it is." Jonathan chuckled at the police detective's questions.

Jim looked up from his notes at Sarah, whose mouth just gaped open as she realised that this guy might have been trapped for decades and didn't know it. The paramedic tapped the window next to the office door flanked by security, but he waited before entering. Jim said, "Ok, Jonathan, I will leave it at that for a minute, and we can chat later. These medical guys are here to take you to the hospital for a check-up. Sarah will go with you in the ambulance, just to help explain a little." He nodded to her. She was puzzled; the guy physically was ok, and what on earth could or should she tell him?

Jim, seeing the puzzled look, leant over quickly and whispered to Sarah, "A word outside." They stepped outside with the paramedics, leaving Jonathan to finish his tea and peer around the room. Jim told Sarah, "You stay with him until they settle him down in the hospital, please. I don't want anyone telling him it is 2014 until he is at the hospital at least. Have I made this clear?" He flashed a look at the paramedics, who hadn't a clue what was going on. "There's always the chance he could panic or have a heart attack or something. Plus, he is relaxed at the minute, and by just letting him talk, we could learn a lot of very valuable information. That's what I need to be fed back to us here, ok? When you're happy, Sarah, can you then come back? I might need to rely on you to do this again if more people are released."

Sarah agreed with a nod. She escorted the paramedics into the office and helped Jonathan to his feet, handing him his stick, which was set in the corner. He smiled at the people all around him after his cup of tea and wondered what all the fuss was about. He joked that he felt like a bit of a celebrity or something with all this attention.

They decided to keep all the relatives out of the main laboratory, but they had them in a nearby room, keeping them close, just in case. It was now getting to be quite a large operation, and extra officers were brought in to keep order. Obviously, the relatives were keen for news of what was going on, and in the absence of facts, rumours had to be dismissed and some kind of managed waiting game developed for them all. There were also the practical things. like drinks and food. The situation could easily get out of hand.

The press had a sniff of a story and were now trying all sorts of tricks to gain entry. The police set up two perimeters, one letting the relatives in and keeping the press outside completely, and the other keeping everyone out of the main forensic lab itself. They had to keep a real lid on this. While Jim was dealing with Jonathan, Lesley set up small teams to watch the mirror on a rota basis, and Josh set it up so the mirror could be recorded twenty-four seven.

A few hours had passed after Jonathan Steedle had been released, and Sarah had now returned to the group from the nearby hospital. She reported back to the group that whereas Jonathan was physically fine, mentally was a different matter, as he had missed eighty-seven years. A call came from over at the mirror, and Jim and Lesley quickly made their way to it, as did some of the others.

The mirror's patterned mosaic look had changed again, just like before when Jonathan had been released. Once again, the mirror's surface revealed one large view of a single room, this time with a woman in it. As the mist cleared away, the room it revealed this time looked more modern than the one before, with bright colours and a small telly on the corner table. The woman looked young, around her mid-twenties, and she was black, maybe of afro-Caribbean descent. She was slim, with a huge afro, and she was dressed in a new psychedelic mini dress. You could tell it was a new dress, because the label dangled from the back of her neck as if she had just been trying it on, perhaps at the time she had disappeared into the mirror.

She seemed to be in a good mood, humming a tune as she walked around the room, appearing to get familiar with her surroundings, which was a bit surreal after possibly being in the room for many years. Lesley guessed from her attire and the room decor that she could be from the sixties. All they needed now was for Austin Powers to burst in with a "Yeah, Baby!"

As they watched, the young woman froze to the spot, her eyes wide, as the voice loudly boomed the words, "I AM AIAKOS!" Just like Jonathan, she too immediately looked to the ceiling corner of her room.

Like before, the voice continued, "YOU ARE NUMBER 15501. IT IS TIME FOR YOUR JUDGEMENT. STATE YOUR NAME!"

As before, all in the laboratory were glued to the proceedings. The woman looked terrified, and shaking, she quietly mumbled, "Tier... Tier Missoni."

There was a minute or two of silence, and then Tier jumped as if she'd had an electric shock as the voice continued once more, "THE MIRROR HAS BEEN BROKEN, AND SO HAS THE BOND. YOU MUST NOW BE JUDGED!"

Tier, in a frightened voice, said, "But I didn't break any goddamned mirror, you fool. What are you talking about?" She had no reply from the voice, and again, she shouted, "Hey you! Mr Keeper!" Still nothing.

The laboratory teams gathered expectantly. The lady in the mirror, like Jonathan, seemed to be just the other side of the glass – so close. But, at least, this time, they had an idea of what was likely to happen and were more prepared. Members of the team had worked quickly and efficiently, googling her name and coming up with information.

She had been twenty-five years old when she'd disappeared from her flat in London, where she'd worked as a waitress in a fashionable club. The bar owner, a Stephen Crain, had been convicted of her death, although the body had never been found. The evidence had showed previous beatings she had received at his hands, and after her disappearance, her diary had convicted him, stating how he had raped her and how she had feared for her life and so couldn't go to the police. The jury had come to the conclusion that she had done just that, plucked up enough courage to finally go to the authorities, and then had been killed by him to keep her silent.

He'd served a twenty-five-year sentence. He'd been refused parole many times because he wouldn't reveal the location of her body to the grieving relatives, who were relentless in their pursuit of justice and their desire to find her body. He'd been thirty-five years old when convicted and sixty when released in 1990. He'd died at the age of eighty-two in a care home, still hounded by the relatives asking the whereabouts of Tier Missoni's body, which, of course, he couldn't have known. She had a younger sister, who'd been thirteen years old when Tier had disappeared, but of course, that had been in 1965, so bizarrely, she was now sixty-two-years old. She still lived in London, and her name was Isobel Jacobs.

Jim said, "Ok, can we get her sister down here as quick as possible?"

His instructions were cut short, however, by the voice of Aiakos. "YOU, TIER MISSONI, UTTERED THE NUMBERS AND WERE CAPTURED BY THE MIRROR; THE MIRROR'S BOND WAS BROKEN. YOU HAVE NOW BEEN JUDGED."

"TIER MISSONI, YOU ARE NOW FREE TO LEAVE. GO AT ONCE!"

Those in the laboratory hurried out of the way again. It was Lesley who remained the closest, as, hopefully, a woman's face would be far less frightening as Tier exited into the laboratory. As Tier slowly emerged from the swirling mist of the mirror, her eyes seemed even larger than before, if that was possible, looking so bewildered at the assembled group.

Lesley offered a hand and said, "hello, Tier. It's ok. We're police and medical personnel. You're quite safe now. Don't be afraid. We're here to help you." Lesley guided her on through the smiling group to Sarah, who, like before with Jonathan, took her on through to the office where she could settle a moment while waiting for the paramedics to collect her.

Trevor told Jim he had just gotten off the phone with her sister, Isabel Jacobs, who would make her way to meet her at the hospital. Tier overheard part of the conversation and asked, "Can I talk to her? She will be worried about the hospital. She is only thirteen years old. Who's going to be with her?"

Trevor couldn't answer her, but his eyes gave away that something was wrong when he tried to gesture to Jim as to what he should say. Jim, realising, stepped in and said, "It's ok, Tier. Isobel has someone with her."

Tier looked puzzled, and she said, "There's something very strange going on. Why did you call her Isabel Jacobs? Her name is Missoni! What's happened? Is she okay? Has she been hurt? Why is she going to the hospital?"

Sarah got her into the office, sat her down, and tried to reassure her that her sister was fine and that it was just that they wanted her to go to the hospital to get checked out, and that meant her sister would meet her there. Thankfully, the paramedics were now there at the door of the office. Sarah stayed with her, and they all went off to the hospital together.

Jim and Lesley gave a collective sigh and then returned to look at the mirror. As expected, it had returned to the rows of boxes. Like before, there were no gaps where the empty boxes had been – they noticed that although two had now gone, the others were all simply slightly bigger to fill the frame. Jim also noticed that the other empty boxes and the ones that had had dead people in them were also gone.

Jim, like Lesley, had been there in the laboratory for many hours. He needed sleep. They had lost all concept of time in the strange world of the laboratory. It was as though they were nearly in their own time zone. He once again had Jessica on his mind as he set up a makeshift bed on her office floor. He made it to one side of the now quiet office. It felt uncomfortable, and even though it was near midnight, sleep would not come easy. His mind wandered and drifted. It wasn't as though he had been in a relationship with her for years, but they had gotten together, and he felt partly responsible for her, especially after she had put in so much work on this case. It was even her place of work that he was now lying in. As Jim began to doze off, he wondered how long it would be until she too would be released from this crazy situation. He was just marginally comforted by the fact that those who had just been released seemed remarkably well, totally unaware that they had been inside a mirror for any length of time. Bizarrely, he kept thinking, *Aiakos*, as he finally dozed off.

In the quiet of the night, outside the office and across the laboratory, a half-asleep security guard "watched" the mirror with instructions to raise the alarm if anything about it changed. His shift had been barely two hours long, but sitting there, staring at a mirror, wasn't very exciting. As he failed to maintain his vigil, the mirror' surface began to silently swirl with mist, and the square rooms faded until, for the third time that day, the image displayed in it had changed into that of one single room.

Chapter 14

Ben Stevens had been watching the mirror, but as can happen when you stare at an object waiting for it to do something, he had not been fully aware, almost dozing off at times. He jolted awake as someone coughed in the room, and he was suddenly thrown awake and now looking not at a row of box rooms in the mirror, but at a single room which filled the mirror's frame. He shouted to the others, sounding, perhaps, a bit panicked. In truth, it was just the fact that he had startled himself awake and then realised he had nearly missed something.

No one noticed, though, that the tone of his voice was down to him being startled into belated action. Josh knocked on the office door where Jim was dozing, but he jumped awake at the breaking news that the mirror was doing its thing again.

Jim asked straight away, "Is it Jessica?"

Josh shook his head. "Sorry, Jim. No, it's a guy. I think it could be that journalist chap that we thought may have broken into the laboratory."

Jim's heart sank with disappointment. He'd had the feeling it could be Jessica this time, probably because he had been thinking of her before dozing off. He shook his head, trying to wake up fully, and stumbled to his feet and into the main laboratory, following Josh, who was now at the mirror.

Sure enough, as he reached the mirror, he recognised the guy standing before him with hands on hips, coughing up half a lung. It was the scruffy-looking Dennis Presswick that they had previously been looking for.

After a short wait, they again heard the now-familiar, booming voice of Aiakos announcing himself. "I AM AIAKOS!" The mirror frame shook slightly with the volume.

Josh mimicked with a mocking, "I am Aiakos, woooooer!" Jim glared at him – things were far too serious for joking – and his glare was quickly grasped, with Josh stopping his talking and giving an apologetic look back.

Jim's concentration didn't wane with the minor distraction, and he was now fully focused on the room in the mirror. It was, of course, the laboratory that they were all standing in and from where Dennis Presswick had disappeared. This made for an even stranger aspect thrown into the mix. Dennis, still standing, looked a bit puzzled at the voice that had just proclaimed itself as "Aiakos". He didn't reply at first but waited to hear any further dialogue; after all, as far as he was concerned, he had just blagged his way into the laboratory and didn't want to give away anything at the moment.

The voice said, "YOU ARE NUMBER 553. IT IS TIME FOR YOUR JUDGEMENT. STATE YOUR NAME!"

Dennis coughed his horrible hacking cough and said, "I am Dennis. Who are you?"

"STATE YOUR FULL NAME!" boomed the voice.

"NO," answered Dennis. "Why should I? I know my rights."

The voice boomed out, "553, STATE YOUR NAME NOW!"

"I told you. Dennis... cough cough."

The voice continued anyway, "THE MIRROR HAS BEEN BROKEN, AND SO HAS ITS BOND. YOU MUST NOW BE JUDGED!"

"You don't scare me," replied Dennis. "I'm with the Associated Free Press. I know my rights." He coughed again; sweat trickled down his now red face.

"YOU, DENNIS PRESSWICK, UTTERED THE NUMBERS AND WERE CAPTURED BY THE MIRROR. YOU HAVE NOW BEEN JUDGED!"

Dennis again interrupted, saying, "There you go; you know my name anyway, so why fucking ask me!" He pause for an answer, and when none came, he continued, "You can't bully me." Once again, there was silence.

All those waiting in the laboratory moved slightly into position for when he was released from the mirror. They waited, but the pause seemed longer than before. Dennis broke the silence with, "Ok, ok, I blagged my way in here. So what, I didn't break in, and I was escorted in. Phone the police if you're that bothered, 'cos I ain't!"

After another long pause, the voice of Aiakos returned to the room. "DENNIS PRESSWICK," it snarled, "YOU ARE GUILTY, GUILTY OF CAUSING THE DEATH OF LUCY FERNELLE."

Jim and the others' relaxed demeanours froze and then changed to puzzlement. They looked at each other, and someone said, "What?" It was Josh. He said, "Wasn't she that singer who died a few years back? Wasn't she?"

Dennis was surprised for once, and he thought a second before answering so that he was a lot slower to respond than in his previous exchanges with Aiakos. He eventually came back with, "I think you have made a mistake, whoever you are. She committed suicide. Everyone knows that."

Aiakos kept quiet. Meanwhile Jim, Lesley, and the rest of the police team flew into action. "Is there anyone from his family or friends from the press here in the holding room?" barked Jim. H turned to Trevor and Simon and said, "We need info on her death ASAP!"

Lesley agreed with the actions and confirmed that there was a guy around in the other room from the press association. She knew because he was the only person connected to Dennis that they would let in, and even then, it was with strict rules not to speak to the others. He was here for Dennis, nothing else. She'd even selected people for him to be next to in an offshoot of the main holding room. So Lesley decided the press guy would be her task. She didn't want info going to him; she wanted info from him, and he was bound to be suspicious.

Jim momentarily returned to the mirror. Dennis was still there, one minute with his hands on his hips, the next pacing about and coughing. Jim shouted at the mirror, "KEEPER, CAN YOU HEAR ME?" There was no reply. "MY NAME IS JIM TURNER. IF YOU CAN HEAR ME, I'M HERE FROM THE POLICE. WE WILL LOOK INTO THIS DEATH, BUT DON'T FORGET, WHO OR WHATEVER YOU ARE, YOU ARE ALSO SUBJECT TO BRITISH UK LAW!"

Still, there was no reply, but at least, he thought, it had been stated for all to hear, except possibly Dennis, who obviously was still strolling around his version of the laboratory, oblivious but deep into his thoughts. Jim turned to Josh. "Hey, Josh, you seemed to know a bit about this Lucy Ferrell. I remember she was an American girl, wasn't she?"

"Yes," confirmed Josh. "She was only about nineteen years old. She had a hit song in America and then started to look into acting too. She looked like maybe the next big thing, perhaps, but it was all very early on in her career, and she was hardly known here in the UK. Then I think she came over to the UK a couple of years ago and was found dead in a top hotel in London. I can't remember the details, but I thought there could be something drug related, but we all jump to those conclusions when things like that happen. Anyway, it wasn't my type of music. It was real shit pop crap, so I don't really know anymore, I'm afraid."

Josh was a good lad. Jim thought he had really stepped up to the mark, especially with Jessica away. Josh, yet again, went for a fresh coffee while Jim kept a close eye on the mirror. Before they had finished their cups of coffee, Simon and Trevor returned with some information, their laptops confirming some of what Josh had said. For a start, it was left an open verdict at the coroner's inquest, but her death was strongly suspected of being caused by a drug overdose, and it was not known if anyone else was present at the time. A maid discovered the body in the morning. She had stayed there three nights of a fourteen-night stay.

"The news article was an exclusive," said Simon, "and yes, you guessed it, the journalist who provided it was none other than Dennis Presswick. It was, apart from her celebrity status, a straightforward inquest. She was known to have taken drugs before and had been charged in the States no less than three times before for drugs possession, twice for smoking grass, once for coke."

Lesley returned, and with her was a Martin Stone from the Associated Press. Jim wasn't too keen on him coming through to the main laboratory, but Lesley explained, saying, "Hi, all, this is Martin Stone, Associated Press. It will be quicker and easier if he fills you in on our Dennis."

Martin said, "Right. Lesley has said that someone has accused Dennis of an involvement of some kind in Lucy Farnell's death? Well, in a way, he was involved. He is also a mate of mine, so, cards on the table, he did some near-the-mark snooping. We had heard of the young Lucy coming to London to promote her fledgeling music career, and Dennis is good at blagging his way in places, so he managed to get into the hotel. He didn't, to my knowledge, get into her room and certainly not the night before her discovery that morning. He did, however, get information about a drug contact in she had in London, who Dennis brilliantly managed to catch red-handed as she paid him in the reception area of the hotel. Would you believe it, he even had Jack Keegan, a top photographer, there for the all-important snap."

Lesley chirped in, "How did he get to know when and where?"

Martin continued, "Well, as I said, he is good at blagging. He got hold of someone at the hotel, who dropped off some rubbish from her room for him to go through, and he even managed to get some phone numbers. Lucy begged him not to print what he knew, but Dennis is a pro and stuck it to her, even about how much money she had blown, and he somehow found out she had given the director a blowjob to try and get a part, possibly also getting her out of a 'cash flow problem'. The director denied it after her death, and we couldn't go to print with that bit 'cos she was dead, and the movie director would have turned it into shreds. But who knows, in the future, we may still be able to use that bit. But what I'm saying is, Lucy, at the time of her death, didn't know half of this wasn't going to come out, and at nineteen years old, she was in a right mess.

"The director is married with kids and seventy-two years old, so she was very embarrassed that this could come out, which, coupled with the drugs photo, meant she could face jail, and also, no money must have tipped her over the edge. Dennis was, of course, only doing his job, but as Lesley here told me, you were after someone who was holding Dennis and could mean him harm.

"I'm just saying he was innocent of any involvement in her suicide, but if this nut has it in his head that Dennis is to blame, well, yes, he came up with the evidence to push her that way, but that's just the way this stuff goes! Oh, and on the night of her death, he was in the Crown and Anchor with me until late, discussing the information over a few beers. Plenty of witnesses too!

"Look," replied Lesley. "We're not out to crucify Dennis; we're just in an unusual position here, and I hope all this information is correct, or Dennis could find it more difficult getting out of it."

Checking with Lesley first, Jim got them all together, including Martin, in a huddle and then briefed them. "I've already shouted at this Keeper guy that it is down to us to investigate, so now what we will do is play it that we are opening a new investigation because of new evidence that has come to light, but this would mean the Keeper has to release Dennis for us to proceed further. Ok, that way, if it is for this Keeper to get justice, he may leave it to us." Luckily nothing else had happened while they had been gathering the information and getting organised.

Josh and Sarah, being strictly to do with forensics and not the policing, were keeping watch on the mirror, a little removed from the team huddle. Josh called out to the others, "I'm not too sure, but maybe something is going on in the mirror."

As the rest of them made their way over, Jim took the opportunity to pull Martin to one side. "Now, I'm trusting you while you are here. No fast ones, trying to get a story or whatever. Check with me before you speak a fucking word. Do I make myself clear? Lives could be at stake!"

Martin hurriedly agreed, "Yeah, yeah, no worries. I get the message."

In the mirror, Dennis was puzzled, looking around the room; his demeanour had changed, as if something was happening. His focus now seemed to be on the top left corner of the laboratory, where a swirling mass was developing. This had been the area from where the voice of Aiakos had seemed to emanate from on the previous occasions. The swirling mass turned into a vague, floating image, starting with the figure of the nineteen-year-old Lucy Fernelle. In the image, it looked like she was talking to a man at a hotel reception. Then the images started to clear slightly, as if they were all watching CCTV footage of the scene. As it got clearer, making them feel like they were all there in the reception area with them, a scene unfolded. The guy, who was dressed in tracksuit bottoms, T-shirt, and a baseball cap, also looked young, around the same age as Lucy, twenty years old maybe. He was meeting up with Lucy in what looked like a posh hotel reception. Once security had been waved away by Lucy, in the background, you could make out Dennis sitting there and pretending to be reading a newspaper, shielding the photographer next to him, who was snapping away.

As the scene unfolded before them, they became aware that it wasn't quite what it looked like. The guy in the baseball cap introduced himself as "Zee" to the hotel security. Then, once over with Lucy, he said he was part of a music company in London and that his name was "Philip Jones". He discussed his charity work on a record that could be coming up and then handed an envelope to Lucy, who asked what it was. He said that it was just details of the producer's location and possible timings of a get together, along with phone numbers. Then he said he had a few other errands to run and that his cab was waiting outside and he had to dash. With that, he jumped up and ran outside and into a waiting cab.

Lucy looked about her and then at the envelope. As she opened it, her face completely changed. Inside, there appeared to be a plastic bag with white powder in it, while across the way, as her focus centred on the envelope, the photographer was snapping away like mad. Lucy's head snapped up, a horrified look on her face, as she realised she had been set up in some way.

Tucking the bag back into the envelope and going a little red faced, she quickly covered her hands, swivelled around, looking even more guilty, and headed for the lifts, still being snapped as she ran. She punched at the lift control buttons with her fingers, two, three times, as if it would make the lift come quicker, and then she noticed a rubbish bin next to the lift door. Just before entering the now open lift doors, she looked about, still not noticing Dennis or the photographer, and in an increasingly panicked state, she stooped slightly, dropped the brown envelope into the bin, and then dashed into the lift, just beating the doors that were closing.

Seconds later, Dennis went over to the bin and picked the envelope back up out of it, popping it swiftly into his pocket. He smiled and even chuckled, patting his photographer on the shoulder. "Well done, Jack," he said. "How'd that look on film?"

Jack smiled back as he scanned through the camera's viewer, checking his "perfect job". They walked back outside, and Dennis handed a cash note to the security guard on the door. Then, as he stood outside the hotel on the pavement, the guy Zee, or Philip, turned up and was also handed a few cash notes. Then they all went their separate ways.

In the laboratory, they all looked at each other, and then in particular at Martin. He straight away protested his innocence, saying, "I had absolutely no idea it was a fit up!"

Again, their attention was brought back to the mirror image of the laboratory. Dennis, instead of being apologetic shouted, "So what! So it wasn't nice, but it didn't kill her!" The only reply was silence. Then the swirl of an image appeared in the room he was in. It cleared, as it had done before, to reveal Lucy, this time meeting Dennis. Because the two were dressed in different clothes and it was in her hotel room, Jim and the others assumed it was a future date and time after the previous scene.

Lucy was crying, begging possibly, as Martin had mentioned before, asking him not to publish the photos. She pleaded her innocence. Dennis looked smug. "Sorry, my dear. These photos don't look innocent, and along with some more information I've got about you getting some money to 'blow' – or should I say from a blow? – I think I too could make a bit of cash here. Now, have you got the money, dear?"

Lucy produced an envelope, a white, fat-looking one. Dennis opened the end and thumbed through it. A moment later, he said, "This doesn't look like ten thousand to me. It's nearer to five grand."

Lucy blubbed again and begged and pleaded for more time. "It's all I have."

"Well," said Dennis, "let's just say half the cash means maybe only half the information comes to print. Your choice, my dear, the drug deal or the blow job on the seventy-two-year-old director?"

The picture image they were watching from the forensic laboratory changed again to Lucy on her own in bed, drinking and then reaching for a needle, which she placed into her arm. Then she lay back on the bed, drifting away, as did the image before the assembled group and, of course, Dennis. Jim, Lesley, and the others rounded on Martin, who was now blurting, "Honest, I didn't know. I swear!"

Lesley said, "Well, sorry, I don't believe you. Who was it that said about the blow job? Quote: we might use the information at a later date? Why did you say that? Was it because you were going to extract money from the director too?" She didn't wait for an answer to any of these questions; she was just letting rip at him, voicing everyone's disgust, and as Dennis wasn't there, he would do for now.

"Trevor," she said, "can you read this gentleman his rights and ask someone to drop him down the station, please, to be investigated and possibly charged with manslaughter, bribery, blackmail, extortion, aiding and abetting all of the above, and withholding information from police. Take this lowlife out of my sight NOW!"

Their attention, as he was led away, was brought immediately back to the mirror and a now very differently perceived Dennis Presswick. After what they had just been shown, Jim asked the question, "Is this Keeper just a vigilante? Have we been tricked in some way?" Everything was getting so confused and frustrating.

Chapter 15

Dennis carried on, shouting up at the area where the voice and clips had been shown, protesting that it had to be proved, but this was just met with more silence. The time passed, and it still wasn't clear what would happen. They hoped that Dennis would be released into their custody swiftly so that they could deal with the odious man.

Then, as they watched, they saw the corner of the ceiling area in the mirror's laboratory start its swirling mist again. They waited for the voice, as did Dennis, but there was just silence, and then a cascade of what looked like small brown leaves fell from the swirling cloud of dark mist.

Dennis stepped back. He seemed extremely disturbed at the event. The cascading continued like a waterfall, pouring from the corner. Dennis looked frightened then as he moved further across the room, away from that corner. They could see the brown material had landed in a heap on the floor and was spreading out slowly.

As the material moved across the floor, a few particles flew back up for a meter or two and then landed again. The investigation team members were absorbed, trying to work out what was going on. They soon became aware of a low humming sound, which seemed to grow in volume.

Trevor called out, "Cockroaches."

"Yes," said Josh, "I think you're right."

Jim commented, "What do you think, Lesley?" She was puzzled and said little, deep in her thoughts at the time.

Dennis backed right away as the cascade stopped pouring from the corner. By now, the flooring in the mirror image was nearly fully covered. He ended up at the centre of the room, at a centre aisle unit with a worktop and sink on the top and drawers and glass-fronted cupboards underneath. Dennis coughed as he went climbing onto the worktop, about a meter and a half at the most off the floor.

The cockroaches roamed around, but they found it hard to scale the glass doors of the units, allowing Dennis a little reprieve from the waves of roaches. The ones that did fly up had no direction and just bumped into things. Dennis moved up the tabletop further, which meant he had a clear two to three metres of room before he got to the sink and drainer.

He swung his legs up out of the way, squirming around, but the worktop was not meant for such a large frame. It was only an inch or so thick, with a hard, white, glossy top. He looked down as his weight started to make it bow, and stretched himself lengthwise as much as he could to spread the weight. He felt a bit easier once he could see the bugs falling back down the glass fronted doors and drawers beneath him.

As he moved around onto his side to look, he felt a sharp prick on his large backside, near his hip. He had accidently jabbed a hypodermic needle into himself. He yelped and immediately pulled it back out, but it was nearly empty of its load.

He panicked. He couldn't, of course, jump down onto the floor, so he had nowhere to go. He had already tried the doors and window, which, strangely, seemed false. The door handles and window latches were like 3-D images, as were the doors and windows themselves, just like pictures, so lifelike that his hands had grabbed thin air before he'd given up.

No, he had nowhere to go. Frustrated, he shouted, "What was in the needle? Did you make me do that somehow, you shit!" There was just silence, apart from a buzzing and hissing. Hissing? The hissing became louder. Dennis still wasn't sure what the hell was happening, nor was the onlooking group from the real lab. They just stood transfixed as the action unfolded before them, all making small observations like how there were no extra roaches joining in and speculating on what kind of drug could have been in the syringe.

They soon noticed that Dennis was moving around less on the worktop and was rubbing his legs, patting them as if trying to wake them up. Had they gone numb? This continued until his legs were still. His arms were now also acting differently, as if going numb too. He shouted out, "I can't feel my legs! Help! Can anyone hear me?" Josh and Sarah guessed at what drugs they knew of that could cause such an effect: paralyse the limbs but leave the head and torso so that he was still able to breathe, move his head, and speak.

Jim said to Lesley, whispering in her ear, "I'm getting really concerned here. This leaves him trapped, paralysed, and very vulnerable. The view seemed to zoom in a little. They could see him breathing, albeit coughing, as he panted. The odd cockroach landed on his face as he lay lengthwise on his back, which showed he couldn't defend himself by brushing them off with a hand. They landed, but flew off again or crawled away as he flicked his head from side to side or blew at them and coughed.

Then, as the buzzing and hissing continued, they heard

another noise, a new sound, which grew louder. More and more frantic, puzzled looks went around the lab group as they watched and listened intently.

Then Josh had an idea. "Hold on. That desk would be that one over there, yeah?" He pointed at a similar desk that was central in their laboratory. Josh ran over to it. Sarah, the only one not to just shrug her shoulders, answered, "Yes, I think your right." She then confirmed her thoughts with, "Yes, because it is further along than the other units to give it more space underneath for..."

She stopped herself from saying it. Jim and Lesley looked at each other, puzzled. Then they impatiently said together, "WHAT?"

"What's underneath, guys?" Sarah also dashed over to their lab desk unit as Josh opened the double glass doors and drawers to reveal a few glass tanks that were long and shallow. In them were a number of RATS!

Josh quickly explained, "Sometimes, we need rats to experiment with. We hold them here, but they don't normally get frantic. What's going on?" It was as if he was thinking out aloud, and he pulled out several drawers, handing them to Sarah. As he looked quickly under the worktop, he noticed a couple of pipes that ran along the underside of the top. Then he remembered the hissing! He shouted to the others, "By the mirror there are water pipes going to the sink!"

Jim looked back at the mirror's image. The roaches had backed away from the flooring around Dennis, and around those units, it looked wet. Scrutinising the scene, Jim could now make out steam drifting up past Dennis and the worktop. Between them all, they worked it out: the hot-water pipe had fractured from Dennis's weight bowing the top and was now spraying the frantic rats. There were a large number of rats in there, and with the hot water playing onto the glass sides, the only exit would be the hard plastic lids. But then where...? Oh my God! The penny dropped, and Jim screamed, "They will burrow up through the work top to escape the hot water!"

Dennis didn't know what the frantic noise was, but then he felt movement below his torso and shouted out, "I can't move! What's happening? I can hear scraping under me!" They all looked on, not able to do a thing. Jim shouted out at the mirror, "FOR THE LOVE OF GOD, MAN, STOP!"

The various noises were eclipsed by the voice that boomed out, "I AM AIAKOS. DENNIS PRESSWICK, YOU HAVE BEEN FOUND GUILTY. THE JUDGEMENT IS FINAL. FEEL MY

JUSTICE!"

With that, Dennis gave out a blood-curdling scream. His limbs were paralysed, but his torso was able to feel, and he felt the movement and then his flesh being bitten again and again. Screaming and screaming, he bucked and wriggled as much as he could, but to no avail; he was doomed to a horrific fate. As all watching gasped, cried, and shouted as a group, their horror cranked up to another limit when their horror-struck eyes witnessed the first desperate rat emerge from his blood-soaked chest. Dennis's bulging skin had finally yielded to the gnashing teeth as it burst through, clearing the path for others. Some twelve or more ate their way through, and the rest followed, wriggling through to their safety. Still alive, Dennis fought until he could struggle no more, and then his eyes fixed as the large rats gnawed on his dead flesh, and he was finally at peace.

Too shocked to look away, too traumatised to look and speak, they saw the wriggling mass of rats and cockroaches devour their victim, now just food to them. The group turned away, hardly able to function anymore. Simon threw up over the floor, unable to hold it back any longer. Sarah and Lesley held each other and cried, with their hands covering their mouths and tears streaming down their faces and over their fingers. Jim, Josh, and Trevor were so traumatised that not a word could or would be uttered, each alone with his own brutally abused mind. They turned, and like the women, they walked away with their backs to the fading scene.

Chapter 16

Eventually, the mirror returned to the more sedate smaller squares, although there was, of course, one less now. Jim, as he had done many times previously, scanned them all to find the one Jessica was in to reassure himself that she was still okay for the moment. Though he could make out her features, she and her room were now once again frozen in time and space. He wondered how long would they have to wait for her to be judged, and now, after the last horrific moments, he had to question whether he was eager for her judgement to come quickly to the fore or not. His mind was troubled as he retired to the office where he would try to sleep.

Tossing and turning, his sleep was certainly not easy to come by. Once it did finally come, it still had no ease about it. Not only were there the horrors of Dennis Presswick's demise, but now, lurking in his dreams, was Aiakos. Aiakos spoke to Jim, but this time, it was no booming voice, more like a whispering torment. "I am Aiakos," it stated. "Are you now starting to understand my judgement? As a detective, how much would you like to know for sure what people have done? Not as some flimsy suspicion from evidence collected for months or even years, but as fact, seeing it played out as an event in front of your very eyes as it all happened. Once captured, their name is uttered as a number, and then you watch what they have done in the past, present, or even possible future. Why should they survive? Why not judge them and wipe them off the face of the planet by using their own cruelty turned against them. After all, they had their chances and choices; their victims had no choice or even a chance in your world. The only reason you don't have a death penalty is that you are never one hundred percent sure, but what if you, like me, could be sure? When you watched Dennis Presswick commit the crime against Lucy Fernelle, I felt your hate, your anger, hoping he would get his own gruesome end. I don't need to prove or justify. I am Aiakos, Judge, Jury, and Executioner." Had Jim just dreamed the words of Aiakos, or had Aiakos, in fact, visited Jim's mind?

After a very restless night, Jim woke. He had probably only had a couple of hours of sleep at best, and after a quick wash, he reflected a little on the events of last night and the death of Dennis Presswick. This was a game changer; someone, it appeared, had just been horrifically murdered in front of them.

Jim and Lesley discussed the incident in the office away from the others. They tried their hardest to separate their emotions from the horrific scene, but as Jim pointed out, the facts were that if what they had seen were true, Dennis had met his end almost entirely at his own hands. To avoid the cockroaches, he had climbed voluntarily onto the worktop, thus injecting himself with the contents of the syringe. The rats had been under the worktop, as they were in the real laboratory Jim and Lesley were in now, so had he been murdered? Or had it been an accident? There was Aiakos's rant, meaning his statements were almost an admission of involvement in the incident. They decided they now would have to be very careful if relatives were around; nobody should have to watch something like that, especially if it was a loved one.

There was a call from the laboratory which indicated another poor soul was about to be "judged". The feeling of apprehension made the walk over different this time. Before, Jim had felt the excitement that Jessica might finally be released. Now the thought of it being her turn to be judged just filled him with dread. He tried not to think negative thoughts and tried to brush aside the slight doubt that there could be something in Jessica's past this Keeper could use to pick on.

When Jim and Lesley did reach the mirror, it was someone they knew, but not Jessica. It was, in fact, their Chief

Superintendent Neville Grieves, pacing up and down. As they had done a few times now, they gathered around, waiting to see what would unfold before their eyes, eyes that had already seen far too much, but like small children peeking at a scary episode of Doctor Who, they couldn't close them to the view before them.

They watched and listened to the scene in the mirror as it began the same way as the previous times. The booming voice now really put the shivers down their spines; Josh wasn't mimicking Aiakos's voice now.

"I AM AIAKOS!" Neville, like the others before him, looked to the same area of the laboratory, a mirror version that didn't have the deceased journalist's remains in it. This version only held the uniformed Neville Grieves, who stood steadfastly to the spot, listening to the voice as it continued, "YOU ARE NUMBER 5331. IT IS TIME FOR YOUR JUDGEMENT. STATE YOUR NAME!"

Neville puffed out his chest and boldly announced, "Chief Superintendent Neville Grieves. Who am I talking to, and what do you mean, judge me? I am here on duty as a public servant." He was answered only with silence.

As he paced about the room, the voice started again. "THE MIRROR HAS BEEN BROKEN, AND SO HAS THE BOND. YOU

MUST NOW BE JUDGED!"

Neville didn't seem to react much; he simply looked up and down shuffled his feet a little. Then he stood still, waiting to see what developed.

The group gathered at the mirror as the voice boomed again. "YOU, NEVILLE GRIEVES, UTTERED THE NUMBERS AND WERE CAPTURED BY THE MIRROR. YOU HAVE NOW BEEN JUDGED!"

The group held their breaths, this time with a lot more foreboding. It seemed a long time, but it was only perhaps five minutes when the voice spoke again.

"NEVILLE GRIEVES," it spat the words out, "YOU HAVE BEEN FOUND GUILTY!"

The group, as a whole, gasped at the words in the now-full knowledge of what those words could mean. Neville looked up and shook his head, not really sure what he had done. He finally found the words to answer the statement, asking, "What are you on about, and who are you to judge anyone?"

Aiakos answered, "JACK GREEGHAN, THE OFFICER, YOU KNEW HE WAS TAKING MONEY AND SEXUAL BRIBES. THEN THERE WAS DANIEL ROSE."

Like before, a swirl of mist and motion changed into a vision, almost like a video clip, showing a constable pulling over a silver Jaguar. The group at the mirror looked on, wondering what the superintendent had been accused of. The scene playing continued with the young officer speaking to the guy in the driver's seat of the car and asking the gentleman if he had been drinking. It looked like a country lane, the area was isolated, and the officer asked for the driver to step out of the car. The driver switched off the ignition and stepped out as asked, and as he did so, he wobbled a little on his feet. Standing at a similar height, just over six feet tall, the officer said, "I think, sir, you may have had a drink. Can you confirm your name, please?"

"Yes," was the reply. "My name is Daniel Rose, Chief Superintendent Daniel Rose, to be exact. I've just been to a function, and I'm driving home. I live in fact just a mile or so further down here at New Acres in Jackdaw Lane. Now, constable...?"

"Umm, yes, sir, Constable Neville Grieves, sir."

"Right then, Constable Neville Grieves, I will remember that name. Are you up for a promotion soon by any chance?"

The constable hesitantly replied, "Umm, I don't know. I would hope I'm showing well at work, sir."

Daniel Rose smiled and looked the young constable in the eye. "Well, okay. I will make sure that tomorrow you will be reassessed. You seem a capable chap. I'm sure a switched-on chap like yourself will go far in the force. Now, the sooner I get on my way, the sooner I can mention your name in the right places, okay?"

Neville Grieves looked again at the superintendent in front of him and reluctantly said, "Okay, sir. You drive carefully. I will follow you to make sure you get home." With that, they jumped into their respective cars and set off down the country lane slowly.

The images swirled and went to a young girl lying in the road. She appeared to have been knocked off her push bike, and her head was bleeding under her helmet. Her leg was broken, and she was crying from the pain. At the scene were bystanders getting help. The car that had knocked her down was a Range Rover. Other adults had dragged the driver out of the driver's seat, and they'd only been stopped from doing harm to him by a police officer in attendance. But people were screaming at the officer that the driver had mounted the kerb in his Range Rover and then swerved back onto the road again, colliding with the girl on her bike. The witnesses screamed, "The bastard is pissed!"

There was quite a mob forming, and they were very angry. The officer tried his best to calm things down, but the crowd got even more fired up when the driver, who now looked about five years older than from the first clip, told the officer he was Commander Daniel Rose.

They could see straight away as he staggered about that he was well oiled, and he then tried to tell the officer in attendance, "Yesh, constable, please just get me out of this." But it was no use this time; the scene was a busy town high street, with dozens of witnesses even to his trying to get out of it. The local bobby at the scene was known to all, and he stuck to his task diligently, immediately reading the drunk his rights as the little girl's screams of pain continued.

The mists swirled again and returned to Neville Grieves in the laboratory. He was again shaking his head. He couldn't really protest his innocence; he had looked away in return for a helping hand up the ladder, and yes, he had also looked away about the detective Jack Greeghan and his exploits. His answer to it had been to simply move him to another area to avoid any negative press and any damage to his own career.

Jim and Lesley, in particular, looked on, very worried, as they had just witnessed the barbaric justice of Aiakos. Neville Grieves continued to pace about in his uniform and black, shining shoes. His badge gleamed on his chest, along with his other force insignia. He continued to look up to where the voice had come from and then down again at his shoes.

The corner of the room's ceiling once again started swirling with a dark, smoky mass, swirling faster and faster. Neville stood back a little, but his gaze was fixed on the motion as if hypnotised. Then it spun faster still, getting lighter in colour until it was like a light in the room. As it continued to spin faster, eventually it was so bright it was difficult to watch. Then it stopped. Neville rubbed at his eyes and blinked. The voice of Aiakos entered the room again, ordering Neville to go to a particular cupboard.

Jim turned to the others in the real laboratory. "Any idea what is in that cupboard, guys?" They looked at which one Neville was heading for, and they managed to figure out which cupboard it was. In the mirror, Neville had opened the same cupboard door as if he were in a trance. The voice then told him to take a bottle out. Josh said, "I'm not sure what is in it, Jim."

Neville took the bottle out and placed it on the side. The voice then menacingly asked him, "ARE YOUR EYES SORE FROM THE LIGHT?" Neville didn't say a word but nodded in answer. The voice then asked him to open the bottle.

Jim and Lesley screamed at the mirror for him not to obey, shouting, "Don't do it! Don't!" He couldn't hear them, and he did as he was told as if hypnotised, unscrewing the lid slowly and placing its lid on the table top.

Then the voice boomed instructions, "POUR SOME IN THE LID." Without hesitation, he did as he was asked, pouring the liquid into the lid until it was filled to the brim. Then, as he set the bottle back down, the voice continued, "NOW USE THE LID AS AN EYE WASH."

Again, trance-like, he did as he was instructed, bringing the lid up, turning it as he dipped his head, cupping his right eye and then straightening up. There was still not a sound from Neville, and his back to the mirror, he set down the lid, with some liquid spilling down his face and dripping off his chin onto the floor. As soon as it made contact with the floor, it bubbled and gave off a misty fume. The voice carried on, "Now the other." Topping up the lid again, he set the bottle down as before and picked up the lid, once again filled to the brim. He picked it up and slowly brought it up to his face as he dipped his head, holding it there until instructed to remove it. As he set down the lid, another few drops dripped off the bottom of his face and fell on the floor, its clear liquid fizzing and bubbling as it burnt into the tile. Still facing away from the gathered group in the real laboratory, Neville stood to wait for the next order.

Aiakos boomed out, "YOU, NEVILLE GRIEVES, HAVE BEEN JUDGED. YOU WERE FOUND GUILTY. YOU WILL LEAVE HERE. YOU ONCE TURNED A BLIND EYE. NOW YOU HAVE BEEN JUDGED. YOU WILL ALWAYS TURN A BLIND EYE!"

With that, Neville turned, and Jim and Lesley screamed in horror. Neville's eyes were now deep hollows, still smouldering. As he stumbled towards the mirror, Jim shouted for the team to get the paramedics. They rushed in just in time as Neville finally stepped through the swirling mist of the mirror and into the comforting hands of the group. The team helped pass him onto the paramedics. He wasn't a few seconds into the room before the pain erupted in his eyes and the burnt streaks where the liquid had run down and dripped off his chin. Now Neville screamed, "MY EYES! MY EYES!" He was quickly given over to the medics, who immediately doused his face with water to dilute the liquid that Josh had now identified as concentrated sulphuric acid. The mirror had returned to its rows of box rooms; again, their heads were in turmoil.

While there was a quiet period, they decided to try and sleep. Jim wondered if Aiakos would come into his sleep, but despite it being difficult to achieve, Jim eventually welcomed it. He needed it, and it enveloped him like a comfy blanket. He slept for probably only a few hours, but it was so, so needed.

The next morning eventually came around, and they all had dragged themselves into the lab with a mixture of coffee, teas for some, and a drag on a cigarette for others. A few bacon rolls were offered around, but everyone in the group was running on empty after the last few eventful days. Jim looked in the toilet mirror, and the face that looked back at him was rough: bags under his eyes and stubble on his chin. He brushed his teeth, which made him feel a bit more human, and with his hand, he brushed back his hair, which was fairly short, making it a bit more presentable. If things were not concluded soon, a shower rather than just a wash would be desperately needed. At last count, there was around six rooms or boxes left in the mirror. Each time someone was released or died, another room disappeared, and its space was taken up by the remaining rooms.

Jim had seen Jessica a few times, now frozen in time, awaiting her judgement. It was a strange feeling, not knowing whether he should be happier she was still waiting or if being judged before getting down to the last rooms would be better in some way. Simon and Trevor had a background now on all the remaining occupants that they could identify, except for one guy who was dressed in a business suit. They hadn't been able to find anything about him so far, and there was also an old lady they had to assume was Audrey Tippens, the woman from years back who had been mentioned before, but her history was sketchy.

Then, of course, there was Kim, who seemed an okay guy. He had no convictions, but he'd had some early trouble with immigration when he'd first come to the UK. Alison Fisher, whose husband had remarried her friend Tanya, had been a teacher, but it was not known if she had done anything wrong. There was also "The Great Alfonso", Peter Wilson. He had unsubstantiated whisperings of complaints from mothers of children, but there had been nothing in it.

After Jim's wash and freshening up, he checked on everyone in the laboratory from their tightknit group. Josh was brilliant; there, on the side in the office, sat a bacon roll and coffee, which Jim started on immediately. It was a good job because, like the previous day, the action started swiftly. A call from the mirror area that "Something is happening, folks" came through to the group, but this time, there were two rooms in view, like a split screen.

In one room, there was the old lady, who they thought might be Audrey Tippens, and in the other room was the young man in a suit, who seemed to be agitated, impatiently pacing up and down as he waited for whatever to occur. The old lady was the opposite; she sat on the edge of her single bed patiently, and it wasn't long before the voice boomed out from Aiakos, which both rooms seemed to hear at the same time, along with the assembled group inside the laboratory.

"I AM AIAKOS!" in both rooms, they reacted by looking up and to the corner of the ceiling, just like the others before them in their rooms. Then, to the guy in the sparse, smart-looking apartment room, the voice stated, "YOU ARE NUMBER 7714. IT IS TIME FOR YOUR JUDGEMENT. STATE YOUR NAME!"

The suited guy shrugged his shoulders, and with a cocky tone, he shouted out, "It's Gilsey!"

Impatiently, Aiakos raised his voice further and abruptly shouted again, "STATE YOUR NAME!"

The man shrugged again, but this time, he toed the line, answering, "Okay, okay, Giles Hill."

There was a pause, and then the same was asked of the old

lady, but the number was different, changed to 531, to which she softly answered, "Hello, I'm Audrey, Audrey Tippens."

Jim waved at Trevor. "Can you get any information on this Giles Hill quickly? That's a London accent, I think, if it helps."

The stage had been set, so to speak, and everyone waited, but they didn't have too long to wait, as something happened: Giles walked towards the side of the room, where a door seemed to open. He then passed from his room into the old lady's room. Both he and the old lady looked surprised.

Giles thought he had been in his apartment flat and would be stepping into an adjoining room. Audrey, in her little cottage, thought she was alone, so for a stranger to walk into her living room seemed weird. Both tried to say that the other had invaded their home. They argued at first and then decided to see what this voice of Aiakos had to say on the matter. Giles shouted at the invisible entity, "Where are we? Are we at my flat still, or this lady's home?"

There was no reply, of course. They had no way of knowing they were captive, both of them, in some sort of mirror-framed time-space anomaly, or whatever the latest educated guess in the laboratory arena was. Trevor rushed back to Jim with some news of the suited Giles Hill; he was a banker who had worked for an investment group, "The Talent Group". They had gone bust in the eighties, and he had been a young upward trader, one of the ones responsible for the poor selling and investments. Thousands had lost their money, and savings and pensions had taken the brunt in particular. The group had been on the verge of going bust when young Mr Giles had disappeared, so he was suspected of fraud, and everyone just assumed he had done a runner with some cash before the collapse.

Watching the interaction of the banker and the old lady. they seemed to have just settled in, for waiting for this "Keeper" to give them an idea of what was happening. The team in the laboratory listened to their conversations; it seemed Aiakos wanted all to know their business.

Giles boasted of how much money he was making as a trader, how he had bought and sold shares, made thousands, and even when, as a company, they hadn't done so well, he had. "Last week," he told her, "I took delivery of my new XR3i," bragging away.

The old lady just nodded and then asked, "What is it?"

Giles looked aghast for all of a second and then carried on, saying, "it's a car, a hot hatch made by Ford, a Ford Escort

XR3i in black with Ricaro seats and a big spoiler on the back. It helps with the thrust and down draught, as does its front spoiler and skirts around the sides."

"The skirts...?" She looked baffled. "Well, you look very pleased about it."

"Yeah," he said. "I'm what they call a 'yuppie'. Young and upwardly mobile, that's me."

The group rolled their eyes at the young arrogant banker bragging to the little old lady. The two continued to talk while waiting, and the old lady inquired, "So who did you say you worked for again?"

"The Talent Group." he replied. "We used to be called the Stratton Group a few years ago, so you might know that name, but we were bought out after its collapse. You know, it was on the news. They went bust a couple of years ago. Some people tried taking us to court when they lost everything."

The old lady said she couldn't remember, but she said she did remember her husband had had his money in a big insurance company before he died. "I think they were called Norton."

"Yeah," said the young banker. "Stratton Group owned

them, but when they went bust, as a group, we cherry picked bits of the Stratton Group and discarded that Norton bit, because they already had another arm of the new Talent Group that would do that bit. They just kept the profitable bit, but the bad debts we just dumped into what was left of Norton's side of things and let it sink. You didn't have all your money in there, did you?" he asked. The old lady looked ashen, her old, tired face suddenly looked worse, and she bowed her head. Giles continued, "Ah, well, I'm sure your state pension will do. You can't have that long to go, really."

Jim and the others in the group looking on into the mirror couldn't help but pass comment. "What a great big YUKIE he is!" said Sarah, and Josh added, "He's a prick!"

They couldn't help but look on, listening as the old lady said, "Would you like a cup of tea, young man?"

"Prefer coffee if you have it, love. Two sugars, white."

She stood up as the objectionable chap took her seat. Her steps took time, partly due to her age but also because of her mood; her mind was in turmoil. As she made the drinks, she was silent, slowly stirring her tea and his coffee. She mulled things over, and then she turned and handed a mug of coffee to Giles. She said, "My husband worked all hours as

I brought up our only son, Jordon. He gradually put his money away, saving up until he retired from the army when he was fifty-five years old. He continued to do jobs for people around the village, and eventually, he fully retired at sixty-five years old. We had an advisor around to talk to us about our money. He spoke to my husband; it was his business, I was just a housewife, and our son Jordon had grown up and moved out years ago to work in Canada in the timber industry. But Gerald, my husband, once he had retired..." Her mind drifted back through the years as she started to sip her tea, stopping only in her rambling to ask if Giles's coffee was okay.

Giles said, "Yeah, cheers, love. Great," as he swigged at it, taking several large gulps.

"My husband, Mr Hill, was a PIG! When he retired, he couldn't cope with not ordering his troops around. He had attained the level of staff sargent. He was cruel. He shouted at me from the time I got up to the time I went to bed. I woke up to fetch his breakfast and then endured the day until the time we went to bed, where he demanded his sexual rights and comfort. He turned into a beast."

Giles looked a little uncomfortable at the story, gulping at the coffee as the old lady carried on talking. "My husband put his money into that Norton Assurance, and I heard the chap tell him, 'If you die, sir, your good lady here, sir, would not only receive £10,000 pounds, but a pension of £1000 pounds for life.'"

The young man interrupted, saying, "Is that all?"

"Well," said Audrey, "yes, that's all, but back then, that was an awful lot of money."

Sipping at her tea, she continued, "Gerald, as I said, was a pig, but when he died, I had a meeting with the bank and decided to pay off the cottage and keep the remainder in Norton Assurance so that I would have a higher income from my capital, which has kept me going these past few years since his passing. So, Mr Hill, you now tell me people like yourself have lost my investment?"

"Uh, yes, love, afraid so. That's the way it goes. Switched on people at the beginning of the collapse took out their money and saved some of the losses, but the rest lost the lot."

"Some bastards threw eggs at my car the other week! It's not my bloody fault; it's just life. A bit tough, I suppose, but that's it. If you're young, you can still hack it. If your old and slow, sorry, but you'll just have to get by, love. What about your son? Has he got money? I could probably do him a great plan to invest in."

The group, listening to the banker, were incredulous at the lack understanding from the arrogant sod. Audrey Tippens continued to sip her tea, quietly pondering her future.

The voice of Aiakos broke her thoughts like a sledgehammer through a brick wall. His voice burst into the room of the little cottage. "YOU UTTERED YOUR NUMBERS AND WERE CAPTURED BY THE MIRROR. THE MIRROR HAS NOW BROKEN, AND SO NOW IS THE BOND. YOU HAVE NOW BEEN JUDGED AND HAVE BEEN FOUND GUILTY!"

Outside the mirror, the team looked at each other, confused at the statement. "Who? Giles or Audrey?"

The voice had fallen silent again; Giles remonstrated, asking the invisible entity, "What are you talking about?"

Then, as if drunk, he staggered and his vision blurred. He grasped for the nearby chair, falling onto it, sweat now starting to run from his head so that his dark hair grew even darker as it got damp. Then it shook, as did his body, like he had a fever.

Audrey picked up the empty coffee mug, walked to her sideboard, and set it down. Giles clawed at his throat, loosening his collar and tie; he was finding it increasingly difficult to breathe, and his words, like his breath, stuck in his swollen throat. He managed to huskily mouth, "Audrey, help me!"

She simply sat back down after setting the mug down on the side. Then she spoke quietly and softly as he gasped and spluttered. "Mr Hill, you see, I hated my husband."

"I don't care," interrupted Giles, his eyes puzzled at her lack of interest in his plight.

She just continued, "I hated my pig of a husband so much that I poisoned him. Mixing it in his drink as if it were just sugar. He, like you, took two spoonfuls, and just like with him, I added the poison along with it. Yes, just like him, you're a poisoned pig."

Giles stumbled off the chair again, but his legs wouldn't support him. White and yellow froth oozed from the corners of his mouth as the muscles in his limbs tightened, knotting up just like his chest as he struggled to breathe. The agony showed on his face as the muscles around his heart clenched. His voice ended up like a long, drawn-out gargle of froth and undistinguishable words through lack of air, until his contorted face froze into a stare as death embraced the arrogant yuppie banker.

Audrey continued to sit in her chair, alone in her room as well as her thoughts.

After a little while, Audrey said as loudly as she could, "KEEPER, I KNOW YOU! I'VE ALWAYS KNOWN YOU! I DON'T FEAR YOUR JUDGEMENT. I HAVE JUDGED MYSELF. I WAIT NOW FOR THE PAIN, KNOWING I DESERVE IT, AND I AM PREPARED FOR IT."

With that, those in the laboratory saw the old lady lean back in her chair, her head shaking as a little sweat ran down her brow. Then she quietly struggled with her breathing before tensing up and finally slouching, her face forming a slight grimace. She too found the poison's pain that she had put into her cup of tea.

As the image of the cottage room started to fade, the watchers in the laboratory were totally silent after another shocking end to their vigil of the mirror and Aiakos's ongoing parade of bizarre events.

Chapter 17

This time, Sarah Wilton had not gone to the hospital to escort someone; she was simply going to visit and then give Jim and Lesley a progress report on those who had already been taken there, especially Chief Superintendent Neville Grieves. His wife, Susan, had been called and should be there already.

Lesley knocked on the door to Jessica's office, which Josh and Jim were using as their place to bed down in between episodes of watching the mirror. Inside, Jim was resting alone while Josh was doing his turn mirror watching.

"Hi, Jim. I hope you don't mind, but I asked Sarah to go to the hospital to check on all of them, and then thought I would come over here. To be honest, after sending her there, I suddenly felt a little alone. Stupid, I know, so I came by for a chat for a bit."

Jim, of course, told her to come on into the room. It wasn't very tidy, with his sleeping bag laid down, a few cushions scattered about, and Josh's sleeping bag, which was on the opposite side of the room on the floor but folded in his absence. Jim sat fully clothed in black trousers and white shirt, but he looked dishevelled, his clothes creased from several days of sleeping in and wearing them, his tie discarded long ago. Lesley, in her top and black skirt, sat down close to him on the floor, and they started to talk about what had happened, not in any depth, but more re-examining how baffling and confusing it had all been and if other than waiting there were another way of dealing with the situation.

Eventually, Lesley said to Jim, "I know you and Jessica had feelings for each other."

Jim looked at her, disconcerted at her claim. "How?"

"Well," she continued, "I chatted to her just before she disappeared. We woman can guess at these things. I've seen the glances between you both. It wasn't hard to see, really." She paused for a moment and then asked, "Jim, I know it isn't professional, but can you give me a hug please?"

Jim hesitated, but he knew he couldn't refuse; it had been such a traumatic few days. Lesley, sensing no rebuff to her advance, moved over, snuggling her head from his left side into his chest, just like she was going to listen for a heartbeat. He instinctively put his arm around her shoulder.

They stayed in this position for some minutes until both had relaxed gently into a comforting sleep. As Jim awoke, Lesley was still in the same position, albeit a little lower, as she had, in her sleep, slipped down. He couldn't help but smell her perfume and the scent of her hair.

He started to think of Jessica and wondered if she would be okay. Lesley stirred after a while, her right hand brushing against his lap.

He rolled his eyes as he looked up at the ceiling, willing himself not to react to her touch. His bladder, being full, didn't help the situation, and neither did her right ear resting against his slight belly, her lips almost touching the top of the buckle on his belt. His mind struggled as he felt the warmth of her breath through the thin material of his shirt, just below his belly button. He could feel himself stirring, feeling his face going red. Jim was now in a race against time, not sure whether to wake her up or risk being embarrassed.

Lesley squirmed, more as a response to his little movements, of feeling uncomfortable and making adjustments. But as he and Lesley both moved, the situation was only exasperated by her sliding lower, her face now resting on his belt buckle and her hot breath directly, gently blowing onto his increasing bulge.

Lesley's hand had also moved so that it was beneath his

bulge, holding his right upper thigh; Jim's teeth ached as he clenched them, and he had to do something! He coughed, clearing his throat, and swivelled, rolling slightly to his left so that his right hip had replaced his embarrassment and his side was now under her head. He gave a huge sigh. This effort was just in time, as Lesley was stirring from the feel of the more uncomfortable hip bone on the side of her head. She woke, and immediately realising her position, quickly adjusted herself and sat up. "Sorry, Jim. Was I making you uncomfortable?" He wasn't quite sure if she had noticed. It was very obvious to him, so he now sat leaning forward.

"Fancy a coffee?" he asked. She said, "Yes, please," so that then became his escape route. quickly jumping to his feet, he shot out of the room, not looking back, desperate to relieve himself in more than one way. As he was coming back towards the office with two coffees, Josh shouted out, "Hey, guys, the mirror is changing again." So, instead of walking into the office, Jim stopped and beckoned Lesley with his head to come out, mouthing "M I R R O R." He then headed across the laboratory to the mirror's area, where the others had gathered again.

As Jim arrived, Josh gasped out loud, showing concern as he

recognised his colleague. "It's KIM!" Kim was now full size in the mirror, and he paced around the small bedroom of Julie Pendleton. Jim handed Lesley her coffee as they stood alongside the others, who had already grown silent. Everyone waited as the voice of Aiakos went through its now frequent patter. But with Kim, it was now easy to understand the room number being 337, which indicated his surname to be LEE.

As had the others, he stated his name for Aiakos and waited to be "judged". After a while, as had happened before, the mist swirled in the corner of the room around ceiling height, which instantly worried them all, as they knew from the previous accounts that this meant a possible showing of a past event. The mist showed eventually a vision of Kim lying on a floor. He seemed younger, and Jim guessed the scene in the vision was from five to ten years earlier, perhaps when Kim had been a student. In the clip, he seemed in distress. He was sweating profusely as he lay there on the floor, hot and struggling for breath. To one side of his head, there was a hole, noted only by a crack of light in the darker area he was situated in. He shuffled further towards it. In the poor light, they could make out his gasps as he sucked the air from the small hole.

The picture, at that point, widened out to show the whole

scene. He was, in fact, in the corner of a shipping container, its ribbed structure and metal side giving away its identity to the onlookers. Surrounding Kim were more bodies, also oriental in appearance, all hardly moving. At Kim's feet lay a young child gasping for air. Kim looked at her at the same time as he looked about him. He was fearful of letting others know he had his own supply of air. The young girl's eyes weekly pleaded help before closing, signalling her failure to stay conscious. Eventually, the clip showed outside the container as the police and ambulance crews went into the container and delved through the bodies. As the finally came to Kim, the rescuers shouted to their colleagues, "There's one alive here! Quickly, get a respirator." Kim cried as the clip was shown. He proclaimed his innocence; he'd been buried alive himself when he'd discovered he was near the small hole in the side that saved him. Aiakos simply let the clip run its course, showing that all were dead from the shipping container except one skinny student called Kim Lee, who had somehow survived.

All looking on were very concerned, knowing how others had been treated, so they feared the worst. They had no choice but to just wait, but as they did, to their surprise, nothing was said, and the mirror swirled and misted over.

Josh was the first to break the silence as the first part of Kim emerged from the mirror. Then, to their amazement and relief, he was standing in front of them, looking fine and in one piece.

Josh jumped forward, grabbing hold of Kim in a bear hug. Kim was very confused. To him, it had only been a day, at the most, after he had disappeared. He stood in Josh's arms, looking uncomfortable with the attention, like the Pepe Le Pew cartoon cat being held tight by the skunk who thought it was another female skunk. Josh quickly explained that Kim had been missing a considerable amount of time and that they were worried.

The mirror, still misty, swirled, not settling back to its dormant state. Then the voice of Aiakos boomed out, "NUMBER 337, KIM LEE, YOU HAVE BEEN FULLY JUDGED. WAIT AND VIEW THE MIRROR AS IT SHOWS YOU YOUR CHOICES". With that, it showed Julie Pendleton's room again, but this time, the twelve-year-old girl stood peering around.

She still stood there in her birthday clothes, a small party dress. It was plain blue with yellow piping, and her hair was tied back in a ponytail, just as it had been before her disappearance. Then, as they all watched, the mirror's view changed to a split screen showing a second room: their laboratory, with "The Great Alfonso", Peter Wilson, standing in its centre, looking bewildered.

All in the group looking on were puzzled. Aiakos hadn't said anything more after talking to Kim, who apparently wasn't in the clear yet and had, like them, to watch the latest proceedings as they unfolded. Lesley quickly asked Jim whether Julie's parents should be allowed in.

Jim decided it would be best to bring them in, just in case Julie was freed, but that they should keep them just a little further back from the main group. In the waiting room, Clive and Sandra Pendleton were briefed that some kind of contact had been made with their daughter, but negotiations were at a delicate stage in an effort to get her released.

Entering the main laboratory, they made their way over, flanked by two security guards, to stand behind the main group of detectives, forensic staff, and paramedics, who kindly pointed out to Clive and Sandra their daughter. They all focused in again on the mirror, and the two parents cuddled into each other as they saw their daughter, who appeared unharmed as far as they could tell. As they all watched, the door to her bedroom was opened, and in through it from the adjacent room walked Peter Wilson. He had come from the laboratory room next to hers.

As he entered her bedroom, the door slammed shut behind him. They all could hear him introduce himself to the young girl as Peter Wilson, "The Great Alfonso". Julie was, of course, a little confused that a strange man had just walked into her room, but Peter put her mind at ease with a few silly magic tricks before sitting on the bed next to her. The emotions of those watching were going up and down like a rollercoaster ride, as they'd been relieved to see her relatively well but had also been worried that she was trapped alone. Then they'd briefly felt good that Peter Wilson had gone into the room, thinking he might be able to protect her against Aiakos. But as they watched, they started to become uncomfortable with the way he seemed to be chatting with her, and the fears leapt up further as his hand wandered to her knee while she chatted with him.

Even at twelve years old, you could see she knew this wasn't good, and she tried to jump up away from his grasp. From his pocket, he produced a glinting metallic object, which they soon recognised as a scalpel, presumably from the lab he had just been trapped in.

Julie's parents lurched forward, but they were restrained by the two security men. As any parent would, they desperately wanted to protect their daughter. After being held back, Jim asked them to stay calm a second if they were to stay.

Jim secretly, for the first time, was willing this so called Keeper to do something. if this Peter Wilson was about to harm the child, Jim knew that, standing outside the mirror, they couldn't do anything. He struggled with his thoughts as the drama unfolded in the mirror.

Chapter 18

The room was very small, especially having an adult as well as a child in it. The small bed still dominated the area, with its One Direction bedcover prominent. There were boxes of toys, games, and books to the side, and on the wall were a couple of pictures of the singer Harry from the same group.

Peter Wilson, "The Great Alfonso", moved like a predator around the bed, for he was a predator, a sexual one, and now he didn't hide the fact as he circled his prey. He had picked up the scalpel from the laboratory for protection when he'd moved to this other room, unaware of what he might face. His sick mind had woken up to the fact that an advantage was there to be taken, as he was under the impression that no one would know, just the girl and himself. In a room with no witnesses, her story would be her word against his. There would be no real evidence. He would get away with it. After all, he had done stuff before and gotten away with it. He then reasoned to himself that he could be stuck in this room for a while. It could be quite entertaining for him; he would be looking after her in his own way.

The group watched, frantic to do something, as the

paedophile moved in on his victim. For the first time, he showed the blade to Julie, and the fear in her eyes brought a fresh anxiety from the parents and group watching, who couldn't do anything to help the vulnerable girl. Julie now sat on the bed, facing the large adult, who stood in front of her. He seemed to be single-handedly fumbling with his trousers, eventually producing his penis through his fly. Dangling it at her face level, he now quietly coaxed her, "Touch it."

Julie looked up at him, frightened, tears running down her cheeks, her shoulders moving with her tiny sobs. Peter carried on, saying, "It will be okay. It will just be like a lollipop. There's a good girl. I won't hurt you, but you must be a very good little girl."

All who watched wrestled with their emotions as the scene unfolded. The little girl's parents were now almost throwing themselves at the mirror, but they were held back by the security guards, who were now struggling to keep order as best they could. In the confusion, the general noise increased to a crescendo, but then everything stopped – the scene in the mirror had frozen.

As the group realised this, they too fell quiet. The silence was only broken by some low voice they hadn't realised was talking; it was Kim, mumbling, and as their attention switched to him, the mirror's image swirled.

Kim was reciting his number, 337, which had sent him into the mirror in the first place. In a trance-like state, he slowly walked to the mirror, which was only a few paces away. The group parted to allow him access, and he soon disappeared back into the mirror. The mist then cleared again to reveal exactly the same scene. Sandra looked away at first, but then she turned her gaze back again. Even though it was abhorrent to her – as was it to all – she had to see what was happening.

The scene was as before, except Kim was there now, walking up to Peter Wilson and the young girl, who were static, as if they were some sort of wax dummies. Peter still stood in the same position in front of Julie, his penis exposed, his right hand extended under her chin and holding the scalpel blade to her throat.

Kim jumped as the voice of Aiakos boomed out. "NUMBER 337, KIM LEE, YOU HAVE A CHOICE. YOU HAVE TAKEN THE FIRST STEP, DECIDING TO RECITE THE NUMBERS. WAS IT TO HELP A CHILD THIS TIME? IN ONE MINUTE, THE ACTION WILL MOVE ON, AND THIS MAN WILL BE YOUR ENEMY WITH A WEAPON. AT THIS MOMENT, YOU HAVE AN ADVANTAGE. USE IT!"

Kim looked again at the scene in front of him. He immediately prized the scalpel out of the man's hand. Then he stood slightly to Peter's right. As suddenly as the scene had frozen, it woke up when Kim had the blade in his own hand.

As soon as Peter Wilson was aware he had movement, he thrust forward, only then looking down at his right hand that had been holding the scalpel, unaware that Kim was behind him until Kim, not really sure what to do, shouted at him, "STOP NOW! LEAVE HER ALONE!"

Startled, Peter went to move, but Julie, also startled, bit down, hard. Peter screamed in pain and shock. Kim, confused, went to grab hold of Peter, probably to pull him away from Julie, but with his hand holding the blade, all he succeeded in doing was to plunge the scalpel into his neck, catching his jugular, and blood spurted everywhere. Peter continued to scream, his one hand went to his neck and the other to his crotch, pulling at it.

Julie had released her jaw, but the head of his penis hung by a thread, and blood poured from the open wound. As he staggered around, all three of them seemed in shock. Peter fell to the floor, blood pumping as he shook, and eventually became still in the widening red pool.

Kim dropped the blade onto the floor, stunned. Looking at Julie, he asked if she was okay. She sat stock still on the bed, blood running down her chin. Kim checked the body that lay on the floor, and he quickly established that "The Great Alfonso" was definitely dead.

The voice of Aiakos boomed out: "NUMBER 337, KIM LEE, you uttered your numbers. YOU HAVE NOW BEEN JUDGED AND ARE FREE TO GO. LEAVE NOW!"

Kim looked over at the mirror's glass wall, which had started swirling, then at Julie, who sat on the bed. He rushed over to her, grabbed her hand, headed for the mirror, and dived through, but when he reached the other side with everyone gathered, he no longer had Julie's hand in his. Looking back from where he had come, he was very disappointed to see no sign of her until the swirling mist subsided to show Julie Pendleton still trapped in her room.

Kim felt like he had failed and apologised again and again to her parents, who thanked him for trying, and at least he had saved her from "that beast".

Julie sat on the bed, still in shock. She started sobbing quietly again as she looked down at the bloody remains of the man who had abused her. She then heard a noise.

Scared again, her heart pounding, she whipped her head around to see what was happening. The door had opened, but nobody stepped through. Eventually, she got up, and shaking, she walked over towards the doorway and then through it, finally walking out of her room.

Chapter 19

Another day had gone by, more scenes had played out. and as a group, they were feeling exhausted, both physically and mentally drained. With all the horror, along with people being released, it had been a rollercoaster ride for them all. The mirror had continued to mist and not show what was happening; the new day would hopefully bring about some kind of resolution. Eventually, mid-morning, the shout went up that the mirror was changing! It swirled as the group waited for it to clear. Probably, most expected to see Julie Pendleton.

But, no, it was a woman, one whom they recognised from her picture: Alison Fisher. She paced what looked to be the bedroom she had gone missing from, dressed only in her underwear – bra and pants – probably what she had been wearing when she'd disappeared, trying the clothes on before planning to go to work all those years ago. With nothing on her feet, she padded about, not sure what was going on until, just like the others before her, she heard the voice of Aiakos.

"NUMBER 351, STATE YOUR NAME."

"Alison Fisher," came the puzzled reply, and just like the others, she was told by the threatening voice to wait to be "judged". She waited as patiently as she could to see what was going to happen.

Jim and Lesley had a quick chat and called on her ex-husband and his wife, Tanya Fisher, to come into the main laboratory. Jim had an idea. When John and Tanya walked into the laboratory, they were greeted by Jim and Lesley, who tried quickly to explain that Alison had been found but could be under threat and her life in danger.

Jim suggested that it was up to John and Tanya. With their surnames being Fisher and the room showing in the mirror being their old bedroom, there could be a slim chance that one or both of them could pass through into the mirror. If they uttered the numbers 351, which seemed to relate to their surnames, the 3 being "E" the 5 being "S" and the 1 being an "I", they might be able to enter and help Alison.

John and Tanya agreed to help. It was really them being backed into a corner, driven by guilt perhaps, but they would have looked so bad if they had refused. So John and Tanya stood in front of the mirror, watching Alison pacing around inside the bedroom.

John was the only one to speak as the group looked on. He had a quizzical look on his face as he said, "It's amazing. She looks the same as I remember her from over eight years ago."

Jim and Lesley asked the two of them if they were ready. Although apprehensive, they nodded, Then, together, they chanted the number 351. There was a pregnant pause and silence as nothing happened. Again, they chanted 351. Then Josh pointed at the mirror.

Alison, who had been walking about, was frozen in time and space. She stood with her back towards the bed, looking with a stone-like expression at the mirror, not even blinking. The mirror then misted and swirled as John and Tanya leant forward and stepped into it, with Jim and Lesley giving a look and a sigh, their faces silently asking each other if they were doing the right thing.

The couple walked into the room hesitantly. Not only was there the ordeal of crossing over into a make-believe world of a mirror image – which was difficult enough for them to get their heads around – but there was also the distinct possibility of them being confronted after all this time by Alison, who, all those years ago, they'd cheated on, not to mention the fact that they had no idea how they would explain that they were now married to each other.

In no time at all, they were standing in the room, looking straight at Alison. She stood there like a shop dummy in her undies, Tanya's friend and John's wife. John looked her up and down, shaking his head. *She looks so good*, he thought, but he didn't dare say so to Tanya. Eventually he just said to Tanya, "Now what do we do?"

They didn't have long to wait as Aiakos's commanding voice boomed out once more. "I AM AIAKOS. STATE YOUR NAMES."

They did so immediately: "Tanya Fisher," and then, "John Fisher."

The voice continued, "YOU UTTERED THE NUMBERS, AND IT IS NOW TIME FOR YOUR JUDGEMENT." They looked at each other and came together to give each other support in the shape of a hug and a small peck of a kiss.

The group in the laboratory looked on, wondering what would happen too, and soon, the corner of the room swirled, as had happened before. A short vision started; it was like a short clip montage showing Tanya and John sneaking about, meeting up in cars, kissing and groping. One clip was of Tanya going down on John in his car at a car park and then another was of them both fucking on a kitchen table. Not only were they avoiding Alison, of course, but avoiding Tanya's husband, Rich Blake.

There was one clip showing Rich going off to work and Tanya in bed, waiting for her secret lover, John, who arrived and parked his car around the corner. He snuck up the stairs and pulled off his clothes as he entered the bedroom. Tanya lay in the bed, pretending to sleep. He slid himself into bed beside her, and they talked dirty, turned on by the thought of fucking her on her husband's bed.

As this last image tailed off, Jim and Lesley mentioned that with the previous clips pointing at people's failings, even historical crimes, it would seem that Aiakos was definitely pointing out their cheating, lies, and adultery. Josh chipped in, saying, "It was like watching some sort of porn!" the statement was instantly frowned upon by Jim and Lesley.

Before the clips came to an end, they showed the hard-hitting scene of Tanya finally telling Rich she had fallen in love with John Fisher and was going to leave him. It was very uncomfortable as she told her husband that she not only loved John, but that the sex with him was just unbelievable, even mentioning to Rich that he "just didn't measure up".

The final clip then showed Rich's stone-like face slipping into a noose. The picture expanded to show him in a hotel room, the rope around a larger ceiling beam, his feet kicking away the chair that had supported his weight, and his feet left dangling as his body shook, quivered, and then finally, silently, went still. The death of Rich Blake hadn't been explained to Jim and Lesley, nor the detectives who had quizzed the married couple. Jim and Lesley now voiced their grave concerns with these new revelations.

Judging from what had come before, the visions signalled a brutal punishment soon after by Aiakos.

Alison remained frozen, rooted to the spot, just standing there as the two others, John and Tanya, had nowhere to sit, apart from the bed behind where Alison stood.

They sat down, and as they did, it meant Alison's still-quite-pert bottom was virtually at eye level and only a few feet away from them.

It made for an obvious target to chat about, and Tanya immediately began criticising her choice of underwear. John tried not to stare, but he was a little mesmerised and couldn't help looking just a little bit, to the annoyance of Tanya. Out of their sight and in the far corner of the room, mist swirled, and it then drifted over to them, circling their heads. As they talked, John and Tanya inhaled it.

As the group watched, they could see Tanya's and John's moods change, as if the mist had drugged them or something. John's comments got lewder about Alison's "great looking arse". Tanya started getting more annoyed, climbing onto the bed on all fours. She then hitched up her skirt, exposing her rounded arse with it, her red thong deep in between her cheeks, offering just a glimpse of red, moist material.

John patted her rear appreciatively. The two seemed oblivious to their situation as he then bent forward and kissed both of her cheeks. Then, twisting his fingers under her red thong, he slid them on into her very wet, hot cleft. The scene carried on with John removing his trousers and boxers, showing a very sizeable member that looked hard and ready.

The group glanced at each other, a little uncomfortable. Josh blurted out, "Blimey! Look at him! He has to be nine or ten inches."

Tanya told John to "give it to her", that she wanted it "hard and deep". He didn't pause, pushing into her slow and steady, deeper and deeper until he was all the way in. He then pulled back only to drive in harder.

Tanya squealed, "OMG! That feels massive. You seem bigger than normal. Is it turning you on that your ex, Alison, is standing there and we are fucking literally behind her back?"

John said, "Yes, it is a huge turn on," and he did feel maybe an inch or so bigger for some reason.

Tanya gritted her teeth and hissed a reply, "I want it all, every fucking inch. I want it deep and hard!"

John obliged, thrusting ever faster and harder. Her squeals of delight filled the room as his big cock filled her. But something wasn't quite right. Her squeals were now sounding more like moans of pain, then shouts of pain, and she yelled at him to stop. As the group watched, they were puzzled as to what was happening. They could make out that as John pulled out of her, exposing most of his member but keeping its end inside, and just before he pounded his cock back into her very sore lips, he seemed larger still.

But John didn't stop; he seemed possessed. Faster and harder, he pounded into her, his hands firmly on her hips, pulling her into him as he drove home what appeared to be a monster of a member. It's girth stretched her, as it was increasing in size at the same rate as the length. The onlookers noticed blood coming from between Tanya's legs; she was now screaming with his every thrust.

But, for some reason, John couldn't stop. It was as if he had been taken over. Tanya's screams were terrible, and the group grimaced as he continued pounding. He was now drenched in her blood, staring trance-like while continuing to look down at her bloodied rear as he carried on driving in his monster cock.

Tanya passed out, but John still continued into the lifeless body, pounding away until he eventually gave out a loud guttural grunt as he climaxed. Then, as if awakening from his trance, he looked down at the lifeless figure beneath him. His penis. as he pulled completely out of her. was huge, the size of a baseball bat in length and girth.

Blood flowed from Tanya. She had been split right open, and God only knew what internal injuries had been done, John gently shook her and then checked her pulse. Then his head rocked back on his shoulders as he looked up at the ceiling and screamed, "What have I done!" His monster weapon had returned to a more normal size, and he sat on the bed, his head bowed in horror at what he had just done.

The voice of Aiakos filled the room. "NUMBER 351, JOHN AND TANYA FISHER, YOU HAVE UTTERED THE NUMBERS, AND YOU HAVE BEEN JUDGED. YOUR CRIMES WERE ADULTERY AND THE DEATH OF RICH BLAKE. YOU WANTED TO FUCK HER BEHIND YOUR WIFE'S BACK. SHE WASN'T SATISFIED BY HER LOVING HUSBAND AND WANTED BIGGER!"

With that, from the ceiling, there came into sight a rope with a noose at the end. John looked up, climbed onto the bed, simply placed it around his neck, and jumped off the end of the bed, swinging away from its support.

Alison, still frozen in time and space, stood there next to the bed with no movement at all until a tear slowly and silently ran down her face. The group in the laboratory watched in utter silence as the mirror clouded over and swirled. The group started to turn away from the scene, but then jerked back around as a hand protruded from the mirror, quickly followed by the rest of Alison Fisher. Stepping out, she stumbled and collapsed, not that there was anything physically wrong with her. It was the emotion of what she had witnessed. Although Aiakos had frozen her body with her back to the events, she had still heard everything. Her only saving relief was that she'd been spared the sight of what had happened.

Chapter 20

It was now around four o'clock in the afternoon. The day seemed to be ebbing away. Alison Fisher had been dropped off at the nearby hospital. She was deep in shock and confused. There had been eight years taken away, and then she'd been up from her dormant state to be in a room with her husband and friend who was now her husband's wife! Then there'd been the traumatic ending for both of them. Alison Fisher's head was all over the place, with her feeling alone, guilty, and now, after being taken to the hospital, like the victim she really was.

The team in the laboratory had a bit of a tidy up after the mirror had changed back to the previous state, what they were calling the mosaic state, though this no longer seemed to fit. With just two rooms left, it was now more of a split-screen view, really. It was a hell of a lot easier to watch just two areas, with Julie Pendleton in one room and Jessica in the other, though the team wasn't paying too much attention as they moved around the laboratory.

After the activities had calmed down in Julie's room, she'd walked out of her room, away from the dead body of the magician that lay in a pool of blood. Since then, she'd been walking in darkness, but now, she'd come to another door. She hesitantly opened this second door and walked through it into another room, which was bright white, medical-looking, and in which stood an adult lady dressed in a long, white forensic gown, As soon as Julie walked in, the worried look on the woman's face melted into a concerned, comforting smile aimed at the young child. Julie sighed with relief as she ran to the woman and flung her arms around her. Jessica accepted the big hug, and both were soon crying a flood of tears.

The team was finally alerted to what was happening by Detective Trevor Symmons, who called everyone over to point out that Julie had passed over into Jessica's lab room. Julie's parents, Clive and Sandra, rushed over, having moved away momentarily for the others to clear up, hopefully, for the last two to be released. Jessica was chatting away to Julie; the group couldn't hear them, but it seemed obvious that Jessica was comforting the child, probably telling her all would be ok.

Before their eyes, the image grew until it filled the whole frame of the mirror, covering its surface area as it had done on previous occasions.

Jim and Lesley called in a couple of paramedics to assist, and they all got roughly into a sort of crowded, organised team structure, waiting for what they hoped wouldn't be long before the last two were released. Jim wondered if the two would be released unharmed and if the nightmare would be over. Jessica looked fine, but he did wonder if she would be the same with him. As he gathered with the others, he could feel that the mood had changed from initial excitement to trepidation. Along with Julie's parents and Jessica's colleagues, they all waited, subdued in their manner.

After what seemed like forever, Aiakos spoke. "I AM AIAKOS! STATE YOUR NAMES."

Soon after, there was a reply, "Jessica Lindon," and then a frightened little voice called out, "Julie Pendleton." As she spoke, she involuntarily shivered. Julie quickly whispered to Jessica, "That's him. That's the horrible voice I told you about, and then horrible stuff happened." Jessica cuddled the little girl into her, trying to reassure her, even though, inside, she was also shaking. She felt sick in the pit of her stomach as it churned with nerves and worry.

Aiakos carried on, saying, "JESSICA LINDON and JULIE PENDLETON, YOU UTTERED THE NUMBERS, AND IT IS NOW TIME FOR YOUR JUDGEMENTS."

Then, suddenly, instead of the voice of Aiakos coming from the mirror, it changed and came directly into the real laboratory itself and addressed the waiting group. "YOU ALL STAND THERE WAITING IN JUDGEMENT OF ME AND MY SENSE OF JUDGEMENT! I HAVE SPOKEN BEFORE ABOUT CHOICES. MY JUDGEMENT ON THESE TWO SOULS, JULIE PENDLETON AND JESSICA LINDON, WILL BE DETERMINED BY YOURSELVES THIS TIME. I CAN READ YOUR MINDS, AND I CAN HEAR YOUR CRITICISMS, SO OF THE LAST TWO IN MY DOMAIN, YOU ALL MUST CHOOSE WHO IS TO BE RELEASED, THE GIRL OR THE WOMAN? TOMORROW MORNING AT 8:00 AM, I WILL HAVE YOUR ANSWERS STATED TO ME AT THE MIRROR, AND YOUR JUDGEMENT WILL BE CARRIED OUT, SO CHOOSE WISELY!"

The two in the mirror were oblivious to what Aiakos had said, and of course, they also couldn't hear the group now discussing their possible future lives. The group members stepped away from the mirror and started talking.

Of course, Julie's parents, Clive and Sandra, said straight away, "Surely you will all save the child? Our child?"

Jim stepped in. He didn't want a knee-jerk reaction driven by emotion making the decisions, so he acted quickly. "Right, folks, we have a little time with this. I suggest we try and work towards saving both of them. I will go around you all one at a time, and I don't want to argue. It will waste time. Everyone has a valid opinion. Let's make that clear. I don't want this Keeper to make us condemn someone. If you look at most, if not all, of the deaths so far, it really hasn't been him directly doing the dirty work. I don't want him shifting the moral blame onto us!"

They made a list of all their names and their initial choice. It ended up a bit of a fifty-fifty split, so Jim and Lesley went to each and asked why they had come to their decision. Jim looked at his master list:

Jim – Jessica

Josh – Jessica

Sarah – Jessica

Sandra – Julie

Clive – Julie

Trevor – Julie

Simon – Julie

Kim – Jessica

Lesley – Julie

Out of the nine of them, it was quite a mixed but understandable split. Josh had come up with a good reason for choosing Jessica, apart from knowing her and the fact that she was his boss, saying that if they chose to save Jessica, surely Julie would just be judged as an innocent young child and freed anyway.

Jim said, "Well, this is our initial choice, but I really would like to press that we choose to save them both. Then it goes down on record that we all chose to save them. Then, if he changes that, he can't have a moral way out in some twisted way if his actions do something to either one."

They agreed to sleep on it, but decided as one that they would vote to save the woman and child in the morning. If that got knocked back, they would have to choose one each to save, but they hoped that wouldn't be the case.

It was another uncomfortable sleep-deprived night for them all as they struggled with their decisions, especially the main group, who knew what had been the fate of some of those who had been judged before!

Jim's sleep never really did come; his mind was in turmoil. He knew it seemed like the vote would favour the little girl if this Keeper wouldn't accept both of them going free. His thoughts changed from whether to try and persuade anyone to change their mind to wondering if this Keeper was forcing them to condemn and judge someone to what could be a horrible fate. He dozed fitfully, hearing others moving around and getting up, one of whom was Lesley. He was desperate for sleep, but he couldn't help himself in the end and got up for a coffee and a little chat. He asked her if she was okay.

Lesley replied, "I think so. I'm going through things in my head, wondering if choosing Julie is the right thing to do."

Jim jumped in, saying, "Oh, Lesley, don't tell me you're in doubt. I just can't go talking you out of your choice, and then something happens to the child. We would both be destroyed! This fucking Keeper is clever. He's making it our decision. I hate it. Either way, he will have a decision that is made by us, not him."

Lesley agreed with the whole of his assessment. It wasn't fair to run her decision past him; she would have to back off of that tactic and take her responsibility. She also knew he was right with trying to save both of them. It would ease their consciences if they'd tried their hardest to get him to release both of them.

Lesley said, "Look, I know I came into this later than you, but I think you have done a great job keeping it all together, and who knows, we could still end up feeling that we have saved a life from this nutter, or whatever he is." They finished their coffees and drifted back to their temporary beds, but neither could go back to sleep. Hopefully, though, it would only be for one more challenging night.

Others, too, huddled in little groups or went to their beds tossing and turning. The night seemed to last forever, and when the sun finally rose, Jim knew he would either get his Jessica back with the young girl or he would be agonising as he had done with some of the previous captives. Only this time, if it were Jessica, the stress and anxiety would be multiplied by ten at least.

He washed, shaved, and dressed again, albeit in the same clothes he had been in for a few days now. Then he walked into the arena, not like a gladiator about to do battle, but hopefully not like a lamb to the slaughter either. It was around 7:00 as he entered the main laboratory. The final discussion would be chaired by himself. He had grown more confident in taking control again and fighting off a challenge from the capable Lesley, but with that came the responsibility; he was in charge in every way now. He was now finally going to have to prove it and impose himself on the group in front of him and then on Aiakos.

Jessica and Julie, it would seem, had been placed in a suspended state again while they'd awaited their so-called judgement. Now awake, they walked around the mirror image of the laboratory. Jessica pointed out to Julie where her office was and said, "If you work hard at school, you too can have a career, and it doesn't have to be, say, a nurse; you could be a doctor. A woman can do lots of better jobs these days." She asked if Julie had anything in mind already.

Julie thought a minute and said, "Really, the only jobs I know are being a Mum and a teacher, like Mrs Wilcox, who I don't really like."

"So," asked Jessica, "what do you like at school?"

Julie sighed, looked around, and said, "I don't really like anything. I've hated school from the first day until now. I just want to go home, just like now!" She cuddled into Jessica again, who responded by stroking the young girl's hair, trying to reassure her even though she too was a little worried.

Chapter 21

Jim was dressed in white shirt and black trousers, and he had walked purposefully towards the gathered group; he was ready for, perhaps, the final day of this bizarre episode.

The group stopped their mutterings, waiting for Jim to address them. He didn't falter, as he said, "Okay, well, here it goes. First of all, are we all in agreement that, when asked, we put on a united front, ALL saying we want BOTH freed?" Each nodded in turn. He then went on to confirm it, saying, "Right. That all said, and sorry if it offends, but I don't want anyone to mention, whisper, or mutter about our second individual choices. That's our fallback if things don't work out. Take the lead from me, okay? I don't care how long it takes today. Now, all clear?" All again nodded their approval. "If, somehow, he, this so-called Keeper, doesn't go for both to be released, in some way, each of you will probably have to state your own choices. I will not ask you now for you to decide, and keep it to yourselves for now. When I, and only I, ask for it, you can give it. Are you all clear on that last point?" For the third time, they nodded their agreement.

It was now coming up to 8:00 am, and they stood orderly, as told, silently expectant, like the calm before the storm, perhaps. There was no chit chat, no muttering; they all knew how serious the consequences could be.

The voice of Aiakos said, "I AM AIAKOS!"

Straight away, they saw the reaction of Julie and Jessica in the mirror, so now they knew the two could hear what was going on, unlike the previous day when Aiakos had spoken to the group only about their "choices" they had to make. It meant that when they stated their choices, both Julie and Jessica would know exactly who had voted for whom.

Aiakos continued, and as expected, he gave his instructions: "YOU WILL ALL NOW STATE YOUR DECISION AS TO WHO SHALL BE RELEASED."

Jim quickly held a finger out in an indication to the entire group to hold fire a second. Then he pointed out, one at a time, who was to give their answer first, from left to right.

He pointed at Josh. The big man was a little nervous, being first, and he cleared his throat and started the ball rolling with, "Hi, I'm Josh Slater, and my decision is to release BOTH THE WOMAN AND THE CHILD."

His stated answer was met with silence from Aiakos, which was a huge relief for Jim and Lesley. The only slight, visible reaction came from Jessica on hearing her friend and colleague deliver his answer. She smiled both at its content and at hearing a familiar voice, which was comforting, and in turn, she gave Julie a hug and whispered, "It will be okay. They're on our side. That was Josh; he works with me."

Jim's mind leapt to the totally uninformed and premature conclusion that this could just work. So, sensing that he had an opportunity, he decided to press on quickly to seize the momentum. As soon as Josh had finished, Jim paused for just a moment and then pointed to the next person, who nearly fell over his words, just wanting to get it over and done with: "My name is Kim Lee. My decision is to also release BOTH THE WOMAN AND THE CHILD."

There was still no reply. Jim pushed on even quicker this time, not even waiting for a pause, and pointed to the next in line. Eventually, all had stepped forward and stated that their decision was to release "BOTH THE WOMAN AND THE CHILD!"

Jim was last of all to announce his decision. He stood firm and delivered the same worded statement as the others: "My decision is to release BOTH THE WOMAN AND THE CHILD!"

They looked around at each other, pleased that all had seemed to go okay. The silence began to creep into their minds, though, as they waited for Aiakos's reply. The tension built, and each fidgeted as their anxiety manifested itself in small movements which they fought to suppress. They tried as hard as they could to keep a united, strong front, but the tension grew to an unbearable pitch.

The tension got so thick you could have carved it off the walls with a knife. Finally, it broke as the voice of Aiakos shattered the silence with it's now "usual" booming tone, which seemed louder and more abrupt than before. "YOU ALL HAVE DELIVERED YOUR VERDICTS. THE JUDGEMENTS HAVE BEEN GIVEN AND STATED AS 'BOTH THE WOMAN AND CHILD ARE TO BE RELEASED.' IT IS YOUR DECISION! THIS JUDGEMENT WILL NOW BE CARRIED OUT!"

The group all looked at each other, daring to believe their plan had been a success! Julie's parents smiled at each other, and tears flowed down their faces as they hugged Jim and Lesley, who also gave one another a brief hug. Others sighed loudly and visibly as the tension, fear, and doubt lifted from the room.

They settled back down from the initial high, waiting to receive the two captives as they moved towards the swirling mist of the mirror's glass. Jessica's hand and arm pushed on through and back into the real laboratory. Jim's heart raced as Jessica emerged from the mirror, her other arm trailing, obviously holding Julie's hand.

But Jessica halted her progression out of the mirror with only her trailing hand left on the other side. She pulled at it as if stuck, and she looked puzzled as to what was happening. Julie wasn't following her into reality at all! Eventually, Jessica came on through; her trailing hand not holding on any longer.

Jessica turned, as if attempting to re-enter the mirror, but her access was now blocked. Her hand made a noise as it knocked against the now-solid glass. Julie was, in fact, still trapped. Her parents, Clive and Sandra, questioned what was going on, what was happening, but no answers came. But there were no answers. The whole group was confused.

Just like the group, Jessica too had heard the statements from all of them, and then from Aiakos, that both the woman and the child would be released. The mirror's swirling mist cleared once more, until they all could clearly see the distraught little girl still trapped in the mirror. She moved from side to side, pounding at the glass, walking next to the glass, or just walking around frustrated at her plight.

No one could understand what had happened. Their frustration mounted, along with their fear for the young Julie Pendleton. What was Aiakos up to?

As had happened before, the mist swirled in the mirror again. Then, in the corner of the room, it cleared into a vision. The clip showed an even younger Julie Pendleton at school. She was only around eight years old, and she sat on one of those tiny chairs, painting. The group looked on as there took place in front of them a small disagreement between Julie and a little boy, who sat next to her at the same table, also painting. He was called Peter. The argument was over them dipping their brushes in the jam jar of water. Because they were using different paint colours, the water in the jar soon became a murky, muddy colour. Julie got cross when she used her brush and some of the colours were getting blurred. Instead of a crisp red, she'd put a more burgundy stroke onto the page with her contaminated brush. Julie grumped and whinged at Peter because he hadn't done as the teacher had asked and rinsed out his brush properly before dabbing the paint and changing to another colour. Julie's temper eventually snapped, and her hand swiftly flicked up behind Peter's head, pushing his face down towards his page. But she didn't stop when his head came in contact with the sharp end of his paintbrush. She stood and used her other hand too to push down, and the brush pushed into his eye, causing him to scream with pain.

Julie quickly jumped up and away, and as the teacher came to the boy's aid, Julie stood there denying that she had done anything wrong. "It was an accident," she kept saying, as the seriousness of the situation scared her.

The group looked on as they watched the teacher and the children's parents agree, what looked like sometime later, that it must have been an accident. The vision continued to roll, showing Peter being fitted with a replacement eye, and then the scene faded away again into mist.

The mist quickly swirled and cleared again to reveal Julie, perhaps at around nine or ten years, again at school, which they could tell straight away by the same school badge and coloured jumper. Julie went to a stationary cupboard to collect books for a teacher called Mrs Trenchant. Julie hated her and her history class. As the vision carried on, it showed Julie again going to the cupboard, but this time, from her pocket, she produced a cigarette lighter, and she slowly edged it towards some paper. The vision zoomed in to show her small fingers, with difficulty, manage to push the lighter's little wheel around, delivering its spark to the gas that it emitted. The corner of the paper she held in the other hand soon blackened and ignited from the small flame. Quickly, the paper transformed into flames, and Julie dropped it, possibly surprised at how quick its flames took hold, the swiftness of the results of her actions, and how the act had unfolded. The paper floated down onto the floor, where more books and some small pots of paint were stacked.

The store cupboard was perhaps only approximately three meters deep by two meters wide at any point, but it was extremely cluttered, not only with pens, paper, and books, but a few small amounts of cleaning fluid, paint cleaner, and paint itself. Julie didn't wait to see the effects of her actions, turning on her heels and heading quickly out. Closing the cupboard door behind her, she emerged into the classroom. Only the teacher remained – Julie's class had been dismissed and had gone for their lunch break as Julie had put some books away.

Mrs Trenchant sat at her desk, reading and engrossed in marking work. As Julie left the room, the teacher didn't see her remove the key from the inner side of the door, and as Julie went for her lunch break, closing the door behind her, she silently twisted the key in the lock from the outside. Julie then simply walked down the hall towards the dining hall and dropped the key into one of the small corridor waste bins, walking on as if the actions were no more than closing a door and switching on a light switch.

"Oh my God," said Sandra to the group, "we all thought it was a horrible, horrible accident. The fire brigade said they thought Mrs Trenchant had locked herself in, probably for privacy, because all the children had said she was marking their work when they had left."

Jim asked, "What happened to her?"

Clive answered his question. He could see his wife, Sandra, was very upset, and although shocked himself, he answered, "She was terribly burnt and had to go to the hospital. She later died from inhaling the smoke and flames. It was awful."

The group looked at the mirror, which showed Julie in the laboratory. In the corner, a dark shadowy shape appeared. It grew and transformed into a human-like mass and then glided around the room. It never formed totally into a defined body, but it held a general shape. They knew who it was as it moved over towards the girl from behind and menacingly wrapped its cloak of darkness about her small shoulders.

Clive and Sandra shrieked as calls erupted of "Stop!" and "Let go! You promised!" The figure was now by Julie's side, as if it had an arm around her, guiding her to the middle area of the laboratory. She didn't struggle. In fact, she looked to be in a very calm, maybe even trance-like, state.

Aiakos's commanding voice filled the rooms, both the real laboratory and the mirror version. "I AM AIAKOS. MY JUDGEMENT IS FINAL. YOU ALL ALSO JUDGED AND MADE THE CHOICE THAT THE WOMAN AND CHILD ARE TO BE RELEASED. NOW IT IS TIME FOR JULIE PENDLETON'S JUDGEMENT."

With a rustle of its dark, cape-like shape, the shadow waved at the corner of the room, and it immediately burst into flames. The shape didn't stop there, but turned and waved at the next corner, and it also burst into flames.

The entire group, surprised and shocked by the sudden event, lunged and shouted at the mirror:

"NO!"

"SHE IS TO BE RELEASED! YOU CAN'T DO THIS!"

"YOU SAID!"

"YOU PROMISED!"

There was no distraction; Aiakos didn't falter from his task as he waved at the remaining two corners, and they also burst into flames. As the flames moved towards the middle of the room and, ultimately, the two figures, Julie's face didn't change. She seemed under Aiakos's spell.

The group continued to scream their abuse at the mirror, aimed of course at Aiakos, but it was to no avail. Eventually, the flames engulfed the whole room, with Julie's figure silhouetted against the bright flames, her clothes first and then her hair and skin igniting. The images in the mirror were horrific. Clive, and Sandra screamed, cried, and had to be restrained, but as a whole, they were all shocked and sickened to the core.

As the whole scene was engulfed in flames, Jessica threw up. Tears ran down her face while Sarah tried to console her, as did Lesley. They told her it wasn't her fault as Jessica repeated, "I shouldn't have left her. I'm so sorry." Jim came over to comfort her and to allow Sarah to go to Clive and Sandra. He put his arm around her and confirmed the similar sentiments to her that in no way was it her fault.

Finally, the mirror itself smouldered and heated up in the real laboratory. Jim shouted to Simon and Trevor, "Get a fire extinguisher NOW!" As it smouldered, it gave off an acrid smell. The mirror suddenly cracked, and continued to crack like fork lightening, from top to bottom and then into all angles. The wooden frame darkened until it was black and charred, its joints weakening, splitting, and eventually parting. The glass, fractured already, finally fell, tinkling like a wind chime as the shards tumbled onto the cold, hard tiles, followed with what was left of the mirror's charred, broken frame.

Simon and Trevor used the fire extinguishers sparingly so as not to spray powder everywhere. The fire, though fierce, was concentrated at just the mirror, which sat on ceramic floor tiles, so there weren't too many concerns of it spreading. The mirror was now gone forever, along with the Pendleton's daughter, Julie. The parents were inconsolable as they were led away, sobbing, by the waiting paramedics.

Lesley and Jim helped Jessica to her office. Jim apologised for the mess, but he, like others, had used her office to doss down in until today. Jessica couldn't have cared less about it. She was still mumbling that she shouldn't have left the little girl, asking both Jim and Lesley if maybe she could have saved her.

Jim said, "Maybe we all could have. I really don't know, but it is Aiakos that ended her life, no one else. Now, I think you should go to the hospital and get checked out." Jessica tried to argue against it, but Jim and Lesley insisted.

A few hours later, Jim and Lesley sat next to Jessica's bedside. They chatted to her as her eyes grew heavier and heavier. The doctors and nurses had taken blood, her stats, and all the usual general tests, and then they had left her quiet and calm with her friends. She had insisted they remain until she fell asleep, frightened of being alone after her ordeal. Jim and Lesley had raided the corridor's coffee machine and gotten themselves a drink. Their fatigue was now catching up with them, but their rest would have to wait a while. For now, they concentrated on Jessica, who, as they talked, drifted in and out of sleep, but occasionally, she jumped awake as the horror of the day woke her, pricking her mind just as it dared to try and relax.

The room got quieter and quieter as it got later and later, and all were drifting off. It had been an emotional time. Jim's mind wandered, and the question kept on knocking on his consciousness: *Is it finally over?* He remembered the ashes on the floor of the laboratory, a dramatic answer to the days, weeks, months. Yes, it was over as a drama, but the fallout would probably last an eternity.

The quiet, combined with their drowsy status, was suddenly shattered as there was a loud knock at the private side-room door of the nightingale ward. It was still a very busy hospital, and the hubbub spilt into the room momentarily as Dr Andrews burst in with a young nurse, whose badge gave her name as Amy. She was the friendly nurse who had taken Jessica's stats previously, and she smiled at the assembled group.

Dr Andrews seemed happy, and he almost bounced into the area beside Jessica's bed. He beamed enthusiastically and let out a loud, "Hello," followed with, "And how are we all?" Wisely, he didn't wait for a reply, as Jim looked up a bit miffed at the daft question. But rather than get into a debate with the doctor, he just replied, "We just want Jessica here to be okay."

At the exchange, Jessica woke fully, a little startled as she peered around at all the faces, pulling up her covers around her chin to feel more secure. The doctor, now realising that niceties had been observed, moved on to his patient and spoke to her directly. "So, how are you feeling, Ms Linton?"

She answered, "I'm fine. I think I'm okay. I just feel drained of energy and emotion."

Doctor Andrews bounced again as he said, "Good, good. Well, I have great news. All your tests and readings are normal, and I'm sure if you would like to go home, you can, but I would recommend going tomorrow morning after a good night's sleep."

Jessica said, "Well, if it is okay, I might ask one of my friends to drop me home. I think, although I am dog tired, I would like my own bed. Is that okay?"

"Of course," replied Jim and Lesley.

Doctor Andrews beamed a great big smile. "Okay. Okay. Um, there is one more thing to consider. Is it okay to talk in front of your friends about a private matter?"

Jessica looked totally puzzled. Then she frowned and answered him quickly, "Yes, of course. What is it?"

Again, doctor Andrews grinned, and he bounced about as if he had some affliction. "Well, I should warn you, in your condition, you should get a lot of rest. And, please, no more stress. Take some time off, maybe, if you can."

"What!" said Jessica.

"Yes, Miss Linton, you are pregnant!"

They all looked stunned, but Jim and Jessica were the most stunned. They looked at each other in disbelief, and as if their minds were working in unison, their mouths involuntarily said at the same time:

"The woman and child are to be released."

THE END

Made in the USA
Charleston, SC
31 October 2016